The Duke of Arkholme, a very handsome and very
bored bachelor, organizes a musical Competition to
add some spice to his life and satisfy his love for good
music. But much to the Duke's chagrin, the Competition falls flat...until he is awakened one night
by beautiful music from his own piano, played by an
equally beautiful young woman. From that moment
on, boredom is banished from the Duke's life as he
pursues the mysterious Vanola across England to win
her heart.

A MIRACLE IN MUSIC

A Camfield Romance

Dearest Reader,

This is a new and exciting concept of Jove, who are bringing out my new novels under the name of Camfield Romances.

Camfield Place is my home in Hertfordshire, England, which originally existed in 1275, but was rebuilt in 1867 by the grandfather of Beatrix Potter.

It was here in this lovely house, with the best view in Hertfordshire, that she wrote *The Tale of Peter Rabbit*. Mr. McGregor's garden is exactly as she described it. The door in the wall that the fat little rabbit could not squeeze underneath and the goldfish pool where the white cat sat twitching its tail are still there.

I had Camfield Place blessed when I came here in 1950 and was so happy with my husband until he died, and now with my children and grandchildren, that I know that the atmosphere is filled with love and we have all been very lucky.

It is easy here to write of love and that is why I feel you will enjoy the new Camfield Romances which come to you with *my love*.

Bless you,

Books by Barbara Cartland

THE ADVENTURER
AGAIN THIS RAPTURE
ARMOUR AGAINST LOVE
THE AUDACIOUS
    ADVENTURESS
BARBARA CARTLAND'S
    BOOK OF BEAUTY
    AND HEALTH
THE BITTER WINDS OF
    LOVE
BLUE HEATHER
BROKEN BARRIERS
THE CAPTIVE HEART
THE COIN OF LOVE
THE COMPLACENT WIFE
COUNT THE STARS
CUPID RIDES PILLION
DANCE ON MY HEART
DESIRE OF THE HEART
DESPERATE DEFIANCE
THE DREAM WITHIN
A DUEL OF HEARTS
ELIZABETH EMPRESS OF
    AUSTRIA
ELIZABETHAN LOVER
THE ENCHANTED
    MOMENT
THE ENCHANTED WALTZ
THE ENCHANTING EVIL
ESCAPE FROM PASSION
FOR ALL ETERNITY
A GHOST IN MONTE
    CARLO
THE GOLDEN GONDOLA
A HALO FOR THE DEVIL
A HAZARD OF HEARTS
A HEART IS BROKEN
THE HEART OF THE CLAN
THE HIDDEN EVIL
THE HIDDEN HEART
THE HORIZONS OF LOVE
AN INNOCENT IN
    MAYFAIR

IN THE ARMS OF LOVE
THE IRRESISTIBLE BUCK
JOSEPHINE EMPRESS OF
    FRANCE
THE KISS OF PARIS
THE KISS OF THE DEVIL
A KISS OF SILK
THE KNAVE OF HEARTS
THE LEAPING FLAME
A LIGHT TO THE HEART
LIGHTS OF LOVE
THE LITTLE PRETENDER
LOST ENCHANTMENT
LOST LOVE
LOVE AND LINDA
LOVE AT FORTY
LOVE FORBIDDEN
LOVE HOLDS THE CARDS
LOVE IN HIDING
LOVE IN PITY
LOVE IS AN EAGLE
LOVE IS CONTRABAND
LOVE IS DANGEROUS
LOVE IS MINE
LOVE IS THE ENEMY
LOVE ME FOREVER
LOVE ON THE RUN
LOVE TO THE RESCUE
LOVE UNDER FIRE
THE MAGIC OF HONEY
MESSENGER OF LOVE
METTERNICH: THE
    PASSIONATE
    DIPLOMAT
MONEY, MAGIC AND
    MARRIAGE
NO HEART IS FREE
THE ODIOUS DUKE
OPEN WINGS
OUT OF REACH
THE PASSIONATE PILGRIM
THE PRETTY HORSE-
    BREAKERS

THE PRICE IS LOVE
A RAINBOW TO HEAVEN
THE RELUCTANT BRIDE
THE RUNAWAY HEART
THE SCANDALOUS LIFE
    OF KING CAROL
THE SECRET FEAR
THE SMUGGLED HEART
A SONG OF LOVE
STARS IN MY HEART
STOLEN HALO
SWEET ADVENTURE
SWEET ENCHANTRESS
SWEET PUNISHMENT
THEFT OF A HEART
THE THIEF OF LOVE
THIS TIME IT'S LOVE
TOUCH A STAR
TOWARDS THE STARS
THE UNKNOWN HEART
THE UNPREDICTABLE
    BRIDE
A VIRGIN IN PARIS
WE DANCED ALL NIGHT
WHERE IS LOVE?
THE WINGS OF ECSTASY
THE WINGS OF LOVE
WINGS ON MY HEART
WOMAN—THE ENIGMA

Camfield Romances

THE POOR GOVERNESS
WINGED VICTORY
LUCKY IN LOVE
LOVE AND THE MARQUIS

A Camfield Romance by

BARBARA CARTLAND

A MIRACLE IN MUSIC

A JOVE BOOK

A MIRACLE IN MUSIC

A Jove Book / published by arrangement with
the author

PRINTING HISTORY
Jove edition / October 1982

ISBN: 0-515-06296-0

Jove books are published by Jove Publications, Inc.,
200 Madison Avenue, New York, N.Y. 10016. The words
"A JOVE BOOK" and the "J" with sunburst are trademarks
belonging to Jove Publications, Inc.

PRINTED IN THE UNITED STATES OF AMERICA

Author's Note

The theatre built on the same site in Bow Street, Covent Garden, and which is the present Royal Opera House, was opened on May 15th 1858. The first was built in 1732.

The present theatre saw the establishment of Verdi, Wagner, Puccini and Strauss; also the debut of eighteen-year-old Adelina Patti.

Since the last war the Covent Garden Opera Company has joined with the Sadler's Wells Theatre Ballet, which in 1956 received a Royal Charter from the Queen and became known as the Royal Ballet.

The descriptions of Kate Hamilton's Salon are correct and she was the Queen of London's Night-Life from the eighteen-fifties until she died at the beginning of the sixties.

The Salon, however, carried on and the Shah of Persia patronised it on his first visit to London in 1872. He was reputed to have been an embarrassing guest when at Buckingham Palace he executed a member of his Staff with a bow string.

When this was done the body was buried at night in the Palace Grounds.

A MIRACLE IN MUSIC

chapter one

1860

THE Duke of Arkholme ceased to listen to the rather indifferent performance of an Italian Prima Donna singing an aria from *Faust*.

As a patron of music he found the second rate almost intolerable, and he was continually surprised at the people who had good taste in other directions but were extraordinarily undiscriminating where music was concerned.

He was in fact thinking of whether he should accept the invitation of his hostess, Lady Lawson, to stay after the other guests at her evening Reception had departed.

He was well aware what this entailed.

Lord Lawson was at the moment in the North of England and the Duke suspected that the Reception which had been hastily arranged in the last two days had been entirely for his benefit.

When he arrived to find a small but distinguished dinner-party in the large house in Berkeley Square, the manner in which his hostess greeted him, and the expression in her eyes when she talked to him, made what she intended and hoped for very obvious.

The Duke would have been extremely stupid, which he was not, if he had been unaware that as one of the most distinguished men in England, enormously wealthy and a bachelor, he was not only an exceptional catch from a matrimonial point of view, but undoubtedly 'a feather in the cap' of any Lady who could hold his attention and make him her lover.

That he excelled in the art of love just as he excelled in the hunting-field and on the race-course went without saying, but over the years he had not only grown surprisingly more fastidious but also undoubtedly cynical about his own attractions.

When he sat next to Lady Lawson at dinner she had said in a soft, melodious voice which the Duke had a suspicion was assumed:

"I am hoping, Your Grace, that you will give me your invaluable advice."

"About what?" the Duke enquired knowing what the answer would be.

"I have just persuaded my husband to give me as a present a new Steinway, and as he has complained of its being such an expensive gift, I want to be quite certain that I have the best and it will make the right music to please you."

The way she spoke with a flutter of her eye-lashes and an invitation on her curved lips told the Duke only too clearly that she was not thinking so much of the music pleasing him, but of her own expertise in another field.

He was also quite certain that the Steinway in question would not be in any of the Reception Rooms, but in Lady Lawson's *Boudoir*.

A short time ago he had inadvertently allowed it to be known that he had a piano in the Sitting-Room which adjoined his bedroom in his house in Park Lane.

"When I cannot sleep, which is not often," he had confessed with what he thought later was an unfortunate frankness, "I play to myself the melodies that soothe my mind, and while they are still ringing in my head I find it easy to fall asleep."

Because everything about the Duke was of interest the story flew from one Drawing-Room to another of the fashionable world as if on the wind and was published in one of the gossipy newspapers.

After that every beauty who aspired to attract the Duke told him that she had a piano in her *Boudoir*, and invited him to inspect it.

It was amusing to see how each instrument had obviously been newly installed in a room which had been decorated without thought of music.

In most cases the Duke suspected that the owner of a Steinway or Broadwood was no more accomplished than they had been when they left the School-Room still doing five-finger exercises.

Now, as the Prima Donna trilled on, occasionally slightly off-key on her top notes, which would have made the Duke wince had he been listening, he was wondering whether Lady Lawson's attractions were enough to make him begin a new *affaire de coeur* when he had only just ended another.

He had found as he grew older, having now reached

the august age of thirty-three, that his love-affairs were fiery, tempestuous, quickly ignited and just as quickly extinguished.

He could not explain even to himself why, after a very short time of finding a woman alluring or intriguing, he suddenly became restless and knew it was the first stage of boredom.

At the back of his mind, and on the tongues of every one of his relations, was the question of when, and to whom, he should be married.

Because he had been an only son there were no other direct heirs to the Dukedom, and he was well aware it was his duty to a long line of noble ancestors to produce an heir.

He kept telling himself there was no hurry, and as it happened he never came in contact with young girls.

He was far too astute to accept the invitations, of which he had hundreds, of ambitious fathers and mothers who thought both his title and his wealth would be an agreeable adjunct to their aristocratic lineage.

His interest therefore was always in married women with complacent husbands, and even if they were not complacent they found it best to suppress their jealousy where the Duke was concerned.

They were uncomfortably aware that he could not only outride and outdrive them, but also was a dead shot with a duelling-pistol, should they be foolish enough to call him out.

Although duelling was forbidden by law and certainly frowned upon by the Queen, the Duke had, as it happened, fought quite a number of duels both in England and in France.

He was always the victor and invariably remained unscathed while his opponent spent a miserable two or three months with his arm in a sling.

He was far too expert a shot to wound a man mortally. At the same time it was extremely humiliating for a gentleman who had a real grievance against the Duke to find himself an object of pity to his wife and a figure of fun to his contemporaries.

Lord Lawson was, as the Duke knew, not likely to kick up a fuss if his wife took him as her lover, as long as she was discreet about it.

Lawson was a good deal older than the very beautiful young girl he had married immediately she had made her début, and because his own main interest was in horses he continually left her alone while he journeyed North, South, East and West in order to attend race-meetings at which he won a considerable number of prizes.

It was inevitable that Eileen Lawson should sooner or later lose her heart which had not at all been involved in the spectacular and brilliant marriage she had made from a social point of view.

At the same time, because she was rather frightened of her husband, she was very discreet and the Duke thought it was a point in her favour that although inevitably she would fall in love with him, she would be careful not to cause more gossip than was necessary.

It was impossible to say they would not be talked about.

Because they were seen together, there would be knowing smiles and a certain amount of sniggering amongst the *habitués* of the Clubs who had nothing else to do but gossip about the latest scandal and could ferret out a new love-affair like a terrier at a fox's hole.

However, recently the Duke had been very careful not to involve himself with women who not only lost their hearts where he was concerned, but also their heads.

Because he was invariably by far the most attractive man who had ever come into their lives, they found it difficult to think of anything but love and the fact that he aroused in them new sensations and new emotions they never before knew existed.

The Duke often wondered why other men left their women not only frustrated but also unawakened to the fires of passion.

Because the women to whom he made love always told him he was different from any man they had ever known before and it was obvious that he excited them almost to the point of madness, he could not help knowing that he was exceptional.

At the same time, it made him all the more cautious when it was a question of starting a new love-affair.

As usual he was not swept off his feet by Lady Lawson. He only knew that she was a very attractive woman and that if he touched her the desire he would see in her eyes would arouse a response in him which made it inevitable what the end of the story would be.

"What shall I do?" he wondered. "Shall I stay as she expects? Or shall I make some excuse, and say I have to leave with the other guests?"

It was all too obvious, he thought, what was intended.

As they began to say their farewells he would vanish discreetly into another room and only when the front door was closed behind them could Lady Lawson join him.

Then still keeping up the pretence of having no

other motive, she would invite him to come upstairs to her *Boudoir* to see the Steinway.

The Duke knew exactly what he would find there: shaded lights, and the fragrance of an exotic perfume mingling with the flowers which made the room a bower.

Although it was May it would still be quite cold in the evenings, and undoubtedly there would be a fire burning in the grate beneath some beautifully carved marble mantlepiece on which had been arranged exquisite ornaments of Dresden figures.

He would have no time to inspect the piano which would have been placed in a position where it could not interfere too drastically with the comfortable furnishings which had been there before its arrival.

He would be expected to have eyes only for the occupant of the room, and she would stand looking at him with her blue eyes turned up to his and her lips parted a little as they invited his kisses.

There would be no need to move before she was in his arms, and he would know as he kissed her passionately and demandingly that the half-open door on the other side of the room led into her bedroom, where only a few discreetly shaded candles showed a great bed draped with silk and lace.

The Prima Donna had finished her performance with an aria which was spectacular but certainly not brilliantly performed, and everyone was clapping.

Automatically the Duke clapped too because it was expected of him.

Then Lady Lawson was on her feet and already shepherding her party into the next room where there were flunkeys with white wigs and a somewhat pretentious livery carrying around silver trays on which were crystal glasses filled with champagne.

As the Duke watched her walk ahead of him he thought how graceful she was with her large crinoline swinging from a very tiny waist.

Her neck was long, her skin white, and the diamonds glittering on her fair hair seemed almost like fireflies to entice him.

"She is certainly attractive," he told himself.

Then as she reached the doorway into the Salon she stopped for a moment to speak to one of the servants, and there was a sudden sharp note in her voice which was very different from the way she had spoken previously.

It was in fact as discordant as music that was off-key, and in that second he had his answer.

"No," he told himself, "not tonight, at any rate!"

Twenty minutes later he was driving in his comfortable carriage which he used in the evening back from Berkeley Square to his house in Park Lane.

He had seen the disappointment in Lady Lawson's eyes when he said goodnight long before the last guest was ready to depart, and he knew by the way her fingers tightened on his as he raised her hand perfunctorily to his lips that she longed to beg him to change his mind and stay.

The Duke could however be very ruthless when it suited him, and he was aware that even if she had gone down on her knees and begged him to love her he had for the moment no desire to do so.

Driving away he asked himself why it was that such a small thing should make up his mind for him.

He knew the answer was quite simply that he sought nothing less then perfection.

It was something he feared he would never find,

although just once or twice in his life he had thought for a very short while it was his, only to be disappointed.

As he lay back against the soft cushions of his carriage and raised his feet onto the small seat opposite him, he thought he was not usually so introspective at this time of the night.

But the question in his mind was undoubtedly what it was he was seeking for in life, and what would happen if he ever found it?

He thought now the question arose simply because he was alone and that was unusual.

As was inevitable in his position, he had an enormous number of 'hangers-on.' They were people who made it almost their life's work to interest and amuse him, and whom because he liked them, he counted as his close friends.

Ordinarily he would have driven home from a party with two or three of them to join him in a nightcap.

Unless of course, he was involved with either a beautiful Lady at the house where he had dined, or driving on to where one would be waiting for him, however late he might arrive, he was seldom alone.

Tonight, perhaps because he had anticipated that he might stay with Lady Lawson, he had not asked any of his friends, though there had been several of them at the Reception, to accompany him home.

In fact, he had slipped out before they were aware of it, and he knew they would either be surprised or suppose he had an assignation elsewhere of which they were not aware.

The thought brought back to him the question of what he was seeking and why tonight he had decided not to play the role that was always expected of him.

'I must be getting old!' he thought with a twist of his lips, and wondered if in fact, that was the answer.

Then he knew the reason why he had abstained from doing the obvious was because it was obvious.

"I am sick to death," he said aloud, "of being chased, cornered and trapped by women before I am even aware that I want them!"

That, he told himself, was the real answer to the whole problem of himself and his increasing propensity to become bored almost before he had begun to enjoy himself.

"I should be the hunter, not the hunted."

Now he was frowning and his train of thought was leading him to a kind of anger which his intelligence told him was quite ridiculous, but at the same time was undoubtedly there.

Most men would be only too pleased and proud to be in his position, to own so much, and yet have a different personality and be very much a man.

At the same time he knew the edge of everything he did was taken off it simply because it was all too easy, and there was really nothing for which he had to strive.

For a moment he wondered whether if he attempted to climb peaks in the Himalayas, cross the Gobi desert, or sail up the Amazon it would make him feel any better.

Then he knew that what he was seeking was not a physical achievement, but a mental one, or perhaps the right word was 'spiritual.'

Because that in itself seemed a surprising word to use, he thought it was a long time since he had found any woman who appealed to his imagination, his idealism and his sense of chivalry.

Physically they aroused him, artistically he enjoyed their beauty, but that was all.

"What do I want? What the devil do I want?" he asked aloud and realised as he spoke that his voice sounded somewhat eerie to himself in the confines of the carriage with the horses now drawing up under the portico of Arkholme House in Park Lane.

The red carpet was run down the steps, a footman wearing the Duke's livery opened the door of the carriage, and he stepped out to see in the lighted Hall three other footmen on duty, and his Butler waiting for him.

He handed over his evening cape lined with red silk, his gold-topped cane, his white gloves and his tall hat.

Then he hesitated for a moment and the Butler said:

"There are sandwiches and champagne in the Study, should Your Grace require them."

"I am going to bed, Newman," the Duke replied, and walked up the stairs.

He knew that as soon as he had gone the door would be locked and bolted and the night-footman would take up his position in the large padded curved-top chair by the door.

The lights would be extinguished, except for two or three in the silver sconces, and the house would be very quiet until the first housemaids came bustling to work at five o'clock the following morning.

He walked along the corridor which led to the Master Suite, which had been occupied by the Dukes of Arkholme ever since the house had been built towards the end of the last century.

Because the same Architect, Henry Holland, who had redesigned Carlton House for the Prince of Wales, had also been employed by the Duke of that time, the house was one of the finest in the whole of Park Lane, and certainly the largest.

The austerity of it had mellowed over the years, as the last Duke had had a penchant for gardening.

It was he who had planted the climbing vines, the clematis and wisteria which trailed up the walls at the back of the house, and had added balconies which were now covered with them.

When the flowers were in bloom they not only looked beautiful, but brought a fragrance into the rooms which made those who slept in them think they were in the country.

The Duke however was not thinking of his vast possessions in other parts of England, nor of his ancestral home in Oxfordshire which was magnificent and so large that it was difficult for a visitor to realise it was in fact a private house.

He was still thinking of himself and the impulse which had made him refuse Lady Lawson's invitation tonight, which meant that she was doubtless thinking resentfully, if not plaintively, of him and wondering why she had failed.

His valet was waiting for him and the Duke undressed in silence.

When at last he was alone he blew out the candles by his bed, determined to sleep and thereby rid himself of the cross-examination which came from his own mind.

He knew it was going to be difficult.

Although he had often laughed at people who told him they were unable to sleep and lay awake either worrying or yearning for the unobtainable, he knew that once his brain became overactive, it was hard to drift away into unconsciousness, hoping that tomorrow would bring the answer to his problems.

Not surprisingly sleep eluded him, and he lay in the darkness thinking back over the past.

He wondered if he had wasted the years up until now, and if there was something else he should be doing rather than filling his life with sport and women, with just a sprinkling of politics when he thought it incumbent upon him to attend the House of Lords.

"What alternative is there?" he asked.

He knew uncomfortably that the real answer was marriage, with a wife and family to occupy his time.

That would inevitably mean that he would spend longer in the country than he did now, and certainly would not pass so many hours in *Boudoirs* that contained a new Steinway, or answering the faintly scented invitations that poured into Arkholme House almost every hour of the day.

"Women! Women!"

When he thought about it there seemed to be a host of them besieging him, and he felt as if he fought a battle against them in which, if he was not careful, he would be defeated.

He could almost see himself the only survivor on a tiny hilltop with the enemy surrounding him, knowing that it was only a question of time before his last shot could be fired and he would be forced to surrender.

"Why am I being so introspective?" he said aloud. "Nobody can make me do anything I do not wish to do, and I will not be pressured by women, whether it is to go to bed with them, or marry some flat-faced girl, just because she is a suitable wife from a breeding point of view and will therefore make me a competent Duchess."

The whole idea made him shudder, and yet what else was there except to go on as he was doing now, which for some unknown reason had tonight suddenly turned sour on him?

He turned over restlessly determined to sleep, and when there was no answer to his problem, not tonight at any rate, thinking that in the morning he would laugh at his preoccupation with himself.

He remembered one of his closest friends was coming to breakfast with him, and afterwards they were going together to Covent Garden where he was to judge a Competition he had set up over a year ago to encourage new Composers.

In fact it was the Queen who had said to him that it seemed a pity that England was not leading the world in music in the same way that France and Austria were doing.

The Duke looked surprised.

"I have heard so much about the greatness of Strauss and Offenbach," the Queen went on, "and when Prince Albert and I were in Paris for the Exhibition the air seemed to vibrate with music from the Opera House."

She smiled and added:

"I found Paris the gayest town imaginable!"

"The French are a music-loving people, Ma'am," the Duke had answered.

"So are the Austrians," the Queen said. "And I think it would do us as a nation, good to be a little more musical, and perhaps make us happier."

"You are quite right, Ma'am," the Duke said.

He had in fact, been surprised that the Queen should think of such things, remembering that he thought Windsor Castle was so gloomy and the same might be said of Buckingham Palace.

Then because he was perceptive the Duke thought with a little smile that the Queen was in fact envious.

She had once been a pleasure-loving girl, who had come to the throne when she was only eighteen. She had adored dancing and had always thought of herself as being musical, even though the Duke regarded that somewhat sceptically.

Because he was in fact a great lover of music and gave generous donations to the Covent Garden Opera House every year, he told himself after he left the Queen that what she had suggested was a good idea, and something he would wish to take in hand apart from knowing it was more or less a Royal Command.

The Royal Opera House at Covent Garden had been burnt down twice and the third theatre had been opened two years before in 1858.

The Duke had arranged with the Managers of the Opera House that a Competition should be set up for budding Composers of every nationality so long as their work was original and not yet published.

He would give prizes for their work, which if it was good enough he would see was published and if possible performed.

The idea was hailed with enthusiasm, and the Duke dutifully sent particulars of what was happening to the Queen to receive a letter of congratulations and approval written by her Lady-in-Waiting.

It would be interesting, he thought, to see tomorrow what the second audition of musicians would produce.

The first had been disappointing: there were one or two compositions which he thought would be worth being published with a great deal of work on them, but he doubted that they would win much acclaim.

What he was looking for was something original, sparkling and with that inestimable touch of magic which could not be taught or explained, but which lay in the Composer himself.

The first audition, which had lasted for three days, had been given so much publicity in the newspapers that he was quite certain there would be dozens, if not hundreds, more competitors anxious for a chance of achieving fame.

It would be almost impossible to listen to them all, and he had left it to the Manager of the project to weed out those who were clearly inferior from those that he would hear personally.

'I must discover someone really good,' he thought, but knew it would be like seeking for the ideal woman, and just as difficult to find.

He was now growing a little drowsy, and his thoughts were drifting away into what was a disjointed dream where he imagined he could hear the music he was seeking.

It seemed to seep into his mind and be part of his dream, when he was suddenly aware that what he was hearing was actually being played on the piano in his own Sitting-Room next to his bedroom.

For a moment he thought he must be asleep and dreaming the sound, but as he listened and at the same time opened his eyes in the darkness he knew he was not mistaken.

Incredibly, unbelievably, somebody was sitting at the piano in the next door room and playing a melody that seemed to sparkle on the air with a brilliance that told the Duke it was being played by a master hand.

Because he could still hardly believe his own ears he did not move for a moment, until slowly, still listening, still finding what he was hearing so incredible to be anything but bewildering he got out of bed and groped in the darkness to light a candle.

He almost expected that with the light the sound would vanish. But it was still there, and now that he was free of the curtains which draped his bed, sounded louder.

He found his robe lying on the nearest chair and put it on over his silk night-shirt, listening all the while for the melody from the next room.

Then, slipping his feet into his velvet slippers, he walked towards the door which communicated with his Sitting-Room.

As he reached it and touched the handle he knew he was not mistaken, for the music was not only melodious, but sparkling, brilliant, and although he could hardly credit it, exactly what he had been looking for.

Then he told himself it must be a joke being played on him by his friends, and when he went into the next room he would find them there waiting to laugh at him and expecting him to laugh too.

Instinctively he put his hand up to smoothe down his dark hair, then opened the door almost defiantly.

For a moment he was astonished to see that the room was in darkness except for one candle that stood on the piano.

Then as he looked towards it he could see by its light that there was somebody sitting on the piano-stool.

17

The Sitting-Room was a large one and it was difficult to see in the dim light who was there or what he was like, except that he was still playing brilliantly.

The Duke advanced quietly towards the piano wondering what all this could be about and who his unexpected visitor could be.

Then before he reached the piano he found he could see the performer distinctly and, although it was the last thing he would have expected, it was in fact a woman.

He was conscious of a small, thin, white face and two huge eyes staring at him, and an oval forehead, haloed with dark red hair which in the light of the candle seemed to flicker with little flames.

Then as the music seemed to soften and be played more quietly the Duke found his voice and asked sharply:

"Who are you, and what are you doing here?"

The woman immediately stopped playing to lift something from the lid of the piano and he found himself staring startled and incredulous down the barrel of the pistol she held in her hand.

Before he could speak she said:

"Sit down, Your Grace. I wish you to listen to me, and you have no choice but to do what I ask of you."

The Duke stood still.

"I can only repeat my question," he said. "Who are you, and what are you doing here?"

"I should have thought that was obvious," she replied, with the pistol still pointing at him. "I have been playing to you, and I want you to hear this music which I believe, if you are as musical as you are reputed to be, you will appreciate."

What she said escaped being rude, but there was

18

a note of sarcasm in her voice as if she condemned him for some crime he was not aware he had committed.

Then the Duke, thinking this was the most bizarre encounter he had ever had in his life, said:

"How did you get in here? Unless of course you bribed one of my servants."

"That is a good question," the woman answered, "as apparently bribery is the only way anybody can approach you. Unfortunately, however, I have not the means to grease anybody's palm with gold, and that is why I have been forced to climb up into Your Grace's house."

"You climbed!" the Duke exclaimed.

As he spoke he glanced and saw that the window which led onto the balcony was ajar.

It had not struck him before that thanks to the wisteria and the climbing vines which covered the back of the house it would be possible for anybody of agility to climb into the rooms on the second floor.

At the same time it was quite a dangerous feat, especially for what he realised now was not a woman, but quite a young girl.

"You are certainly trespassing," he said, "and if I call my servants you will be taken to prison."

"I am aware of that," she replied, "and that is why I have come armed. You will listen to me, Your Grace, or you will receive a bullet in your arm, unless by some unfortunate chance I should, by mistake, shoot you in the chest or heart."

"I think perhaps that is a risk I should not take," the Duke said. "I have never trusted females with guns, and I am therefore prepared to accede to your request and listen to you."

"Thank you," the girl said. "I suggest you sit where I can watch you in case you try any tricks."

"Such as ringing for my servants?" the Duke asked. "That is always a possibility before you can get away."

"I will deal with that obstacle when I come to it," she replied. "Sit down, Your Grace, and listen to music which you will not hear at your audition tomorrow because I have not the money to bribe those who are arranging it for you."

There was silence. The Duke did not move, but he merely looked at her.

"Are you telling me that only those who can bribe the Managers of my Competition are heard?"

"Of course I am telling you that," she answered sharply, "and it is something you should have been aware of yourself. Unless a wretched Composer can pay at least five or ten sovereigns for the privilege of having his composition inspected, let alone played, he is sent away and told he has no chance of competing for Your Grace's attention."

The way she spoke was so scathing that the Duke thought that never in his life had he been spoken to in any such manner.

"You indeed surprise me," he said. "I assure you it is something I had no idea existed."

"If that is true, you are very ignorant of the music world in which you think you shine like a beacon. There is nothing but trickery and intrigue. A Composer's work is stolen from him and he has no redress. Usually the only way he can ever be heard is if he pays for the privilege."

She almost spat the words at him and the Duke sat down in the chair she had indicated and crossed his legs.

"You can tell me more about that later," he said. "You have come here to make me listen at gunpoint to compositions that I would not otherwise have heard. Very well, I am listening. Are they your works?"

"No, they are my father's."

The Duke thought she would say more, but instead she put the pistol down on top of the piano and started to play.

First she finished the piece which had awoken him, and which he recognised as an exceptionally spirited rendering of what he thought might be a Hungarian folk-song.

He knew it needed gypsy violins and wild steppes and snow-capped mountains in the background to authenticate its beauty, but such was the girl's skill that her touch on the piano conjured up all those things so vividly that he could almost see them with his eyes as well as hear them with his ears.

When she came to the end of it, she went into what he was aware was a love-song, soft, gentle, persuasive, advancing, retreating and gradually rising to a crescendo of emotion towards the moment of surrender, the climax of rapture.

It was so subtle and so beautiful that the Duke for a moment forgot where he was and was carried away by the music until he suddenly started, as with what was almost a crash of notes the player went into a funereal march, filled with wailing, desolation and loss.

Then as the sound of it became almost unbearably sad there was a softer theme creeping in of hope and faith that death was not the end, just the beginning.

It was so subtly done, so utterly and completely brilliant, that the Duke felt almost as if it was his own thoughts he was listening to rather than music, and at the same time was inspired by it.

Then once again the funereal march came back to the reality of death and the girl lifted her hands from the piano.

For a moment, as if she had been carried away by the music just as the Duke had, there was absolute silence, and neither of them spoke.

Then slowly, almost as if she was coming back from the trance into which her playing had taken her, she turned her head to look at him, her eyes very wide and somehow, her thought, in the light of the candles filled with pain.

"Now," she said, and her voice was hoarse and hardly above a whisper, "do you . . . understand?"

"Why you came here?" he asked. "Of course I understand, and now tell me who your father is, and why, as you say, it was not possible for him to be admitted to my audition."

She did not reply and he went on:

"Surely with a talent like that he could not remain unrecognised?"

"I agree with you, it seems extraordinary," the girl said, "and I have always thought that myself. But you are at the top of the ladder and have no idea what it is like to be at the bottom of it."

The contempt was back in her voice, and the Duke said:

"Let us start at the beginning. What is your name?"

"Vanola Szeleti."

"You are Hungarian!" the Duke said, being sure he was not mistaken.

"My father is," Vanola replied. "He is Sandor Szeleti, and he was well known as a violinist in his own country."

The Duke thought this was what he might have expected and Vanola went on:

"It was however hard for him to make his way in England where, as you are well aware, they are prejudiced against foreigners."

"But I am sure if he plays as well as you do, there must have been people ready and willing to hear and help him?"

"The people we know and who admire my father are not rich men," Vanola replied. "But we existed and were comparatively comfortable whenever he got an engagement in a Theatre orchestra."

"Then what happened?" the Duke asked.

"The cold in this country and the damp affected his hands so that he could not play. They became stiff and swollen."

There was a note of tragedy in Vanola's voice as she went on:

"We thought we should starve, until my mother persuaded him to set down on paper the compositions he had played before his hands prevented him from continuing to do so."

"And you mean to say that these compositions did not attract any attention?"

"No one was interested," Vanola answered. "My mother died, and my father wished only to follow her, and became so ill that he is now bedridden."

For a moment her voice cracked on the words. Then with a superhuman effort at self-control she went on:

"I have copied his compositions dozens and dozens

of times, and taken them to every Theatre. I have played them to Agents and to Managers. Sometimes they have stolen them from me, or suggested that they will only consider them on...their terms."

The way she spoke told the Duke only too clearly what the terms had been, and the horror such suggestions had evoked in her.

"We are desperate," Vanola went on, "desperate to the point where Papa will die of starvation if I cannot make money in some way."

It was then the Duke realised how thin she was.

Because she was wearing a dark gown and there was only one candle to light her in the whole room, he had not realised until he looked more closely that the sharpness of her chin, the thinness of her neck and her hands all proclaimed starvation.

Because he was silent, Vanola looked at him questioningly. Then she said:

"I have come here to ask your help because it is my last desperate chance to save Papa's life. You set yourself up as a Patron of Music, but in fact, you are only pandering to the greed of those who extort money from people who can ill afford it."

She drew in her breath to say more violently:

"Why do you not have the intelligence to understand what is happening in your name? Why do you not see that real talent is being concealed from you, so that sycophants can fill their pockets and laugh at you behind your back?"

Again she was speaking scathingly. Then as if she suddenly realised she was making a mistake she said, and her voice trembled:

"I am sorry...I am being rude...and I did not mean to be...it is only because I am...

desperate . . . desperate to the point where if you will not help me, I think perhaps I will . . . kill you and steal everything that I can from this room, so that I can . . . save Papa's life!"

There was a note in her voice which told the Duke she was not pretending and had in fact reached the end of her tether.

He rose to his feet and as if she was afraid she reached out to take her revolver from the piano.

"I am not going to ask you to trust me," the Duke said quietly. "There is no reason you should do so. What I am going to say is that for me the music you have played to me is absolutely brilliant. It is exactly what I have been looking for but not finding in the auditions I have heard so far."

He spoke quietly, and as he did so she stared at him wildly, as if she could hardly believe what she had heard.

Then when her eyes convinced her that he was speaking the truth, she dropped the revolver on the floor and covered her face with her hands.

chapter two

THE Duke watched her for a moment and as he walked nearer to the piano he said:

"Your difficulties are over now. I can help your father, and I promise you his compositions are so outstanding that with my approval they will bring him a great deal of money."

Vanola did not raise her head, but he knew she was fighting to stop herself from weeping.

Then at last she looked up at him and he thought she was going to thank him, but instead as if a darkness suddenly overtook her she swayed, and before he could prevent it collapsed from the piano-stool onto the floor.

He bent and picked her up in his arms and was aware as he did so that she had fainted not only from nervous exhaustion, after climbing into his house and forcing him to listen to her, but because she was starving to the point where he was certain it was only her will-power which had kept her going.

He carried her across the room and laid her down gently on the sofa, then wondered where he could find her something to eat.

For a moment he contemplated ringing for his valet and summoning the other servants, then decided it would be a mistake.

It would obviously cause a great deal of talk and gossip in the household, and for the moment at any rate he had no wish for his staff to know how easy it was for an intruder to enter the house without anybody being aware of it.

He then remembered what the Butler had said when he returned and walking swiftly from the room he went quietly down the stairs.

As he expected, the night-footman was fast asleep in his padded chair beside the front door.

He passed him in his slippered feet without making any sound, and going into the Study found as he expected a plate of pâté sandwiches under a silver crested cover, and an open bottle of champagne in the ice-cooler.

Carrying them both he went back up the stairs without the footman being aware of it, and when he re-entered his Sitting-Room he saw that Vanola was exactly where he had left her, unconscious on the sofa.

He put down the champagne and sandwiches and lit two silver candelabra on either side of the fireplace, which made the whole room glow with a golden light.

Then taking a glass from a side-table he poured a little champagne into it and knelt beside the sofa on one knee to lift Vanola's head very gently from the cushion on which it was resting.

As he did so he was aware that she was beautiful with straight, classical features, and her eye-lashes were long and dark against a skin that was so white it had the texture of a magnolia.

He saw too the prominence of her cheek-bones, and the lines that came from starvation and privation which ordinarily would not have appeared on such a young face.

As he looked at her, her hair caught the light and he knew it was the glorious red-gold that only Hungarian women inherit and was usually accompanied by eyes that were as green as the trees that covered the foot of the mountains.

For a moment while he lifted her she was still deeply unconscious and her head would have fallen sideways if he had not supported it.

Then he said quietly:

"Wake up, Vanola, wake up!"

As if his voice reached her from wherever her spirit had gone he felt the very slightest response, so slight that it was like the whisper of the wind, or the tremor of a leaf.

He put the glass of champagne to her lips, and when at first there was no response he said:

"Drink! Drink a little, and you will feel better."

As if again his voice reached her, her lips moved slightly and as he pressed the glass against them a small amount of champagne flowed into her mouth and she swallowed it.

"Again!" he ordered. "Drink. It is important."

Now her eye-lashes fluttered and she swallowed the champagne he tipped into her mouth until as it went down her throat her eyes opened and she looked up at him.

He saw they were not green, as he had expected, but strangely dark, almost purple in their depths, the pupils dilated from either pain or fear.

"It is all right," the Duke assured her quickly. "You fainted for want of food, and I have something here for you to eat. But first another sip of champagne will make you feel better."

He was speaking reassuringly, and, as if she understood, she drank a little, then with an effort raised her hands to the glass to push it away.

"No . . . more!"

The words were hardly a whisper, but he heard them.

"Very well," he said. "But I want you to eat, then we can talk. It is important that we do so for your father's sake."

He knew that his words made her make a tremendous effort to sweep away the darkness which had covered her.

Picking up one of the pâté sandwiches the Duke put it into her hand, then rising he set the glass of champagne down on a table beside the sofa and drew up a chair so that he was facing her.

She took a tiny bite of the sandwich, but when it was in her mouth he saw that she found it hard to swallow.

"Eat!" he commanded. "It is what you need. Then we can discuss your future which will be very different from what it is now."

He spoke kindly and quietly as if to a child, and he knew it was her intelligence which made her eat, but her starved body found that after being hungry for so long it was almost impossible to tolerate food.

Slowly and painstakingly, as if she was performing an almost impossible task she finished the sandwich.

The Duke leaned forward and took the champagne from the table and handed her the glass, and she knew without words what he wanted her to do. Then he held out the plate of sandwiches.

"I... I could not... eat any more," she said weakly.

"But your brain knows you should try," he answered, "because we have not only a lot to talk about, but you also have to return to your father."

He saw an expression of fear come into her eyes.

"I cannot... leave him for... long. He is very ... very... ill."

"I understand that," the Duke said. "Tomorrow I will send one of the best Physicians in London to see him."

He thought she would express her gratitude, but to his surprise she said a little stiffly:

"I am not... asking for... charity... Your Grace."

"I am not offering it to you," the Duke replied sharply. "As you know yourself, your father's compositions are the work of a genius, and it seems extraordinary to me that he has not been recognised before now."

"Those who listened to him when he... played knew he was... exceptional," Vanola said, "but because he is an... artist, you will... understand he is also not a... good businessman."

She gave a little sigh.

"Papa never concerned himself with money . . . and people took . . . advantage of that. He left Hungary to play in Paris . . . but while the Concerts in which he took part were a . . . huge success . . . the Manager of them . . . ran away with the leading . . . Soprano and all the . . . money."

Vanola made a helpless little gesture with her hands as she said:

"I suppose Mama and I were very stupid, or rather I was too young to understand that Papa should have had a proper . . . Manager or Agent to . . . promote him . . . but because he was so . . . happy when he was playing and he always seemed to have engagements . . . even if they were not very . . . lucrative ones . . . he never bothered to . . . think about the . . . future."

The Duke thought, having known a number of Hungarians in his time, that it was part of their charm that those who were artistic were never mercenary.

To every Hungarian it was today which counted, and why should he bother about tomorrow?

And yet as he saw Vanola's hands lying limply in her lap and realised that the skin barely covered the bones, he knew that while a Hungarian might have his head in the clouds, it was those who were dependent on him who suffered on earth.

"As I am deeply interested in what you say, and as I think it is going to take some time to hear the rest of your story," he said, "I suggest you drink a little more champagne, and I will join you."

He walked across the room to where there was a grog-tray in case he should wish to entertain his friends there. But it was unusual for him to do so, because he liked to have one room in the house which was quiet and private. So although there was a silver tray with glasses on it, there were no decanters.

He picked up another glass and brought it back to the chair in which he had been sitting, poured himself some champagne, and added a little more to Vanola's glass.

"I am going to ask you to drink with me a toast," he said. "It is a very simple one."

She took the glass into her hand and looked at him questioningly as he sat down in the chair again and he said:

"To the future, Vanola! And may it bring you everything you have ever sought."

He looked at her with a smile, and as if she knew it was what he wanted she raised her glass to her lips and took a tiny sip.

She held it out and he took it from her and put it back on the table.

"When did you come to London?" he asked.

"Two years ago. Papa thought he would get a . . . chance of playing in a . . . Concert that he heard Your Grace was . . . arranging at . . . Covent Garden."

"That Concert was a great success," the Duke answered, "and the proceeds which were very large went towards building a Hospital in which the Queen was particularly interested."

"Yes, I knew that," Vanola said, "and because it was a Hospital for children, Mama and I chose some delightful Hungarian folk-songs for Papa which seemed very appropriate."

"But your father did not play?"

"No. His friend who told us about the Concert said he did not know before we arrived that for those who were not in Your Grace's own list of performers to be included in the Programme involved expending a large sum in bribery."

"Is that true?" the Duke asked harshly.

"Why should I lie?" Vanola answered. "I think that somebody like Papa would have had to find about a...hundred guineas in order to be included and neither he nor his friend had that...sort of money."

"It is disgraceful!" the Duke exclaimed. "I assure you I had no idea of this."

She did not speak but he saw the expression on her face, and he knew she was condemning him for not having been more astute in realising such things happened in the world of music.

Looking back he could see how such a practice could arise.

He had chosen the main performers because they were famous and their talents were undisputed.

The rest of the Programme was given over to those who had been suggested to him by the management of the Theatre, by Impresarios and Agents who continually fawned on him, trying to interest him in one of their protégés.

That they should demand such sums secretly from the artists who obviously could not afford them made the Duke furiously angry, and he was determined it was something that should not happen again.

"After that, Papa...hated England," Vanola went on, "but we could not...afford to leave. He tried everywhere to get work...but because no one had heard of him they were not...interested...and gradually the little money we had began to...evaporate. Then because Papa was...trapsing round from Theatre to Theatre and last winter was very cold...he suddenly developed pains in his hands and could not even play his . . . beloved violin."

Vanola's voice faltered and the Duke realised she was fighting against the tears which came into her eyes.

"I can understand what it meant to him," he said.

"It was . . . terrible!" she said in a whisper. "It was like seeing something very beautiful . . . destroyed in front of one's eyes . . . while there was . . . nothing Mama or I could . . . do about it."

As she gave a little sob and fumbled in the sash she wore round her waist for her handkerchief, the Duke took one from the pocket of his robe and held it out to her. She took it and wiped her eyes with the soft white linen that was scented with Eau de Cologne.

As if she knew he was waiting for her to continue she went on:

"I think it was because Mama was so worried and because she had to be so careful of every penny we spent that she too became . . . ill, and quickly . . . so quickly that we . . . could hardly realise it was . . . happening when she died."

Once again she put the handkerchief to her eyes and when she took it away the Duke said:

"I am deeply touched by your story, but because I know it is putting a great strain on you, I want you to be sensible and try to eat a little more. This time you will find it easier, and unless I am mistaken my pâté sandwiches are very good."

"They are ambrosia after what . . . Papa and I have had to . . . eat lately," Vanola answered, and the Duke liked her courage and the faint smile that came to her lips.

He handed her the plate and she took a wafer-thin sandwich which he knew was nourishing because of the rich pâté with which it was spread.

She ate two mouthfuls, then as if she realised he was waiting she went on:

"Mama died just after the New Year and I knew then that Papa would make little effort to go on living without her. Fortunately before she died she had persuaded him to . . . write down some of his . . . compositions. I made several copies of them although it was difficult to . . . afford the right . . . paper."

She gave a deep sigh before she continued:

"Mama and I had been to Agent after Agent, but none of them was interested and most of them would not even let me play Papa's compositions to them. All they would say was: 'Leave them and we will let you know if they are any good.' But we knew they would either steal them or else throw them away."

She did not speak, the Duke realised, to invite his sympathy, but was merely stating facts, and he knew she thought it was something he should have known.

He was aware that many of the so-called Agents who handled members of the Theatrical Profession were crooked in that they tied young artists to them with contracts from which they could not escape, and deducted very large sums for their services.

It was something about which he had not complained because it seemed a waste of his time, yet now he wondered how many geniuses were lost through such trickery and neglect.

"After your mother died," he asked, "what did you do?"

"I had to nurse Papa, and I also had to have some

money," Vanola replied. "I tried to sell Papa's music, but it was even more difficult than it had been before."

The way she spoke, and the way her eyes flickered and she could not look at him told the Duke all too clearly what had happened.

There would always be men who would abuse their position where a pretty girl was concerned, and who would promise help only if she complied with their desires.

"So you got poorer and poorer."

"We were poor already," she replied, "but when I was reduced to selling Papa's overcoat and almost everything Mama had worn, I knew I had to make one last effort to save him from . . . dying not only from his . . . illness, but from sheer lack of food.",

"That was when you thought of approaching me," he said.

"I heard of your Competition," Vanola answered, "but when I tried to enter Papa's music for your audition, I was told it would cost me twenty-five guineas, or half that sum if I obliged the man who demanded it by becoming his . . . mistress!"

As if the memory of it revived her as even the champagne was unable to do, the note of condemnation was back in Vanola's voice, and her eyes as she looked at the Duke seemed suddenly to flash fire at him as she went on:

"How can you . . . allow such things to . . . happen when you are spoken of with . . . respect as a . . . Patron of Music?"

"It is what I try to be," the Duke answered defensively.

"Music is beautiful, and the expression of the

soul," Vanola said, "and yet you permit those who represent you to wallow in dirt and behave like the devils of hell!"

The Duke thought it was extraordinary that someone so small and frail could speak with such violence.

He knew it was not only because Vanola had personally been insulted, but that music itself was despoiled and defamed.

"I promise you," he said, "this sort of thing will not happen again, not where I am concerned."

"I hope what you are telling me is the truth," she answered. "But I think it may be . . . too late now to . . . save Papa."

"I do not believe that," the Duke said, "and let me assure you that what you have played for me tonight is so immeasurably superior to anything I have heard at any audition so far that there is no doubt at all in my mind that your father will win the prize I have offered for the best musical composer."

She did not speak and after a moment he asked:

"Do you know what the first prize will be?"

"I was . . . told it was . . . 1,000 guineas."

"That is correct, and the second prize will be £500 with five further prizes of £100 each, but those need not concern you."

"And you really think Papa's works are . . . better than those of any other composer you have . . . heard?"

"Immeasurably better!" the Duke replied. "Your father, as you are well aware, is a genius, and I know that not only will I think so, but so will the small Committee of leading musicians who will judge with me tomorrow the final entrants for the Competition."

Vanola clasped her hands together as she said:

"I only hope when I get home that Papa will be

well enough to... understand what you have said. It will make him so happy... not because of the money, but to be... appreciated in England which has... lamentably failed to notice his... existence until now."

"That is something that will not happen in the future," the Duke promised. "And even if your father's gift of playing does not return to him, you will be able to interpret what he has written very ably, as I have heard you do at my piano."

"I only wish you could... hear Papa play his... violin."

She gave a little sigh, and almost beneath her breath said:

"He carries one on... wings up into the... sky!"

"That I can believe," the Duke replied, "and his music made me want to laugh and sing with him. I could see as you played it to me, the flower-filled steppes of Hungary and the snow gleaming white on the tops of the mountains."

"You have been to Hungary?"

Vanola's eyes were very wide and the Duke knew there was a light in them that had not been there before.

"Twice," he answered, "and I thought it was one of the most beautiful countries I have ever visited."

"We should never have left it," Vanola said, "but Papa was excited at the idea of going to France, and Mama thought it good for him to become... famous in other lands besides his... own."

There was a little pause before she added:

"But only when it was... too late did we realise that such ideas were... disastrous!"

"Forget it," the Duke said. "Forget everything but

39

the fact that your father will now be acclaimed in this country, as he should have from the moment he arrived."

"Will you...really do that for him? You do not...think that...tomorrow you will...forget what you have...promised?"

"I have given you my word," the Duke answered, "and although I have many faults, I never break a promise or say something I do not mean."

She looked at him as if she was trying to see deep into his soul, to assure herself that he spoke the truth.

He thought with a faint smile of amusement that it was the first time that a woman had not been only too eager to believe anything he said, especially when it concerned herself.

"Now I must go back to Papa," Vanola said.

"How do you intend to do this?"

She gave him a smile as she moved slowly onto the floor.

"The same way I came. I walked here. It is not far from where we have lodgings."

"And where is that?"

"A street in Paddington."

The Duke frowned. He knew the district was an unsavoury part of London, noted as harbouring more prostitutes than any other.

As if she knew what he was thinking Vanola said:

"The rooms are cheaper there than anywhere else, and after Mama died we could not afford the rather better lodging-houses where we were staying."

"You can certainly not go back to such a place alone," the Duke said.

"I shall be all right," Vanola answered. "And as Your Grace knows, I have a weapon with me which is an extremely effective deterrent."

She picked up the pistol as she spoke which was still lying on the piano.

"I will send you home in a hackney carriage."

He thought actually he should accompany her, but that might cause complications, and to send for his own carriage at this time of night would certainly surprise his household.

"I shall be all right," Vanola said again.

"Leave this to me," the Duke said.

"I have no wish to impose on Your Grace. You have promised me everything I wanted when I came here, and I have no desire to be a nuisance."

"Providing you with a hackney carriage is hardly a nuisance," the Duke answered, "and also Vanola, I am going to give you some money so that you can buy what your father requires until you are formally notified that he is the winner of the Competition."

She had risen to her feet and the Duke knew that she was very still and he was aware what she was thinking.

"I have no wish to be the recipient of Your Grace's charity," she said after a moment, "but I will accept what you give me on one condition."

"What is that?"

"That if, as you have promised, my father wins the prize, the money I take now is deducted from what he receives."

The Duke stared at her as if he could hardly believe what she was saying. Then he said:

"Do not be so ridiculous! Pride is something you cannot afford at the moment."

He said what he thought was the sensible thing to say, but to his astonishment once again her eyes were flashing at him as she answered:

"That might be some people's point of view . . . but not ours. Both my father and mother were very proud people, and it is our pride which has not only kept us alive but kept us believing in . . . ourselves and also that eventually we would obtain justice."

She saw the surprise in the Duke's face and went on:

"That is what I am asking for, Your Grace—justice! And that is why I came to you as I did and forced you to listen to me, because I knew that if Papa received justice his compositions would be accepted at their true value because he is a great artist."

"I agree with you," the Duke said, "and because I also understand your pride I accept your conditions. I will give you £50, which is all I think I have with me now, for your father, and when he receives the thousand guineas, as I am convinced he will, then you can pay me back what I have already given you."

"Your Grace will receive it."

The Duke thought that no Duchess could have spoken with greater dignity.

Now that she was standing up the dark gown she wore showed him how very thin and almost angular her figure was.

The gown was threadbare, and yet it had obviously once been a garment of good taste and he thought she wore it as proudly as another woman might wear an expensive Ball-gown.

Her neck was very long and she held her head high. She was not as small as he had thought her to be when she was sitting at the piano, and although he was tall she had only to tilt her head slightly to look up at him.

As she did so now the light on her hair seemed to

flicker like little flames of fire, and he thought that if she was well dressed and well fed, she would be outstandingly beautiful.

Then, as if somehow the idea perturbed him, he said quickly:

"Wait here while I fetch the money, and I suggest you place the rest of the sandwiches in a napkin which you will find on the table and take them home to your father."

He thought she hesitated and he added almost sharply:

"The food shops will not be open at this time of the night."

"No, of course not."

She walked across to the table in the corner from where he had taken the glasses and the Duke left the room, going to his bedroom.

He always carried a large sum of money with him in the evenings in case there was gambling at the houses he attended, or if the whim struck him to go to one of the Gaming Clubs where he could usually find a number of congenial friends.

He opened a drawer of his dressing-table where he kept the money and found as he expected there were some paper notes and a number of gold sovereigns.

He counted out fifty pounds, and carrying it in his hand walked back into the Sitting-Room.

Vanola was standing waiting for him and she had on now a dark woollen shawl over her head which covered her to below her waist.

Because she was all in black it made her, he thought, somehow more anonymous. At the same time, no woman of any age was safe in the streets at night, especially in the Paddington district.

He held out the money towards her, but for a moment she did not touch it, and he had the feeling she was reluctant to take the money from him.

Almost as if he could read her thoughts he knew she would have preferred to receive nothing until the award was announced.

Then, as if her father's plight made her aware that he should not suffer any longer, she put out her hand and took the money.

"Do you have a bag?" the Duke asked.

"It is safe in the pocket of my gown," she replied.

He realised that in one hand she held the pistol and she stowed the money away, then pulled her shawl closer around her.

"You have not given me your address," the Duke said. "I will pay the hackney carriage that will carry you there, so there will be no need for you to give him any more."

"I think it would be better if I walked, Your Grace."

"With all that money on you?" he asked. "Do not be so foolish! It would be all too easy for some thief to knock you down and rob you, long before you could frighten him off with your pistol."

He had the feeling that she wanted to argue, but as if she appreciated the logic of what he was saying she did not reply.

The Duke walked across the room to open the door into the passage where the candles in the sconces were a little lower than they had been when he walked downstairs before.

Now as they descended the staircase slowly, the Duke deliberately raised his voice, knowing it would awaken the footman sleeping by the front door.

"One day," he said, "I would like to show you my pictures because I feel you will appreciate them, and of course in this house, as in all my houses, I have a Music Room."

It amused him to see how instantly her face turned towards his and her strange eyes seemed to have caught the light from the candles.

"A Music Room!" she said almost beneath her breath.

"And a Steinway which is very much better than the one you were playing upstairs," the Duke said. "When your father is well enough we will give a Concert here and he can play for my friends, including the Princess of Wales, who will appreciate him."

He knew that Vanola drew in her breath.

Then as the footman below them sprung to his feet and quickly pulled his striped waistcoat and silver-buttoned coat into place the Duke said:

"Call a hackney carriage, Henry, as quickly as you can."

"Very good, Your Grace."

The footman unbolted the front door and hurried away and as they reached the Hall the Duke said:

"You have not yet given me your address."

"27 Praed Street, and will you tell whoever brings a message from Your Grace that our rooms are on the top floor?"

She paused before she added:

"It may seem an imposition to ask them to climb the stairs, but I do not think if a note is left at the door we shall ever receive it."

"I might come myself."

Vanola looked horrified.

"Oh, no, you must not do that. Please . . . promise you will . . . not do . . . that."

"Why not?"

She did not answer and he said:

"Are you being proud, Vanola?"

"No, only disgusted that anybody like my father should be brought to such straits, when there are people like yourself at the head of a world in which he should shine like a beacon."

Once again the condemnation was back in Vanola's voice, and the Duke thought with amusement that she never gave up.

"I promise you," he said, "that in the future I shall take much more care to investigate the conditions of any Competition I set up, and the people who administer it on my behalf."

He felt she was not convinced by his answer.

"I will also try to find artists like your father who are neglected or have not the chance to shine as you have put it, like a beacon."

As he finished speaking there was the sound of wheels outside the door and he knew that the hackney carriage had arrived.

"You believe me, Vanola?" he asked.

She looked up at him and he thought once again, incredibly, that her eyes were appraising him, looking deeply and penetratingly into him, as if to be certain he spoke the truth.

"I want to believe you," she replied, "and thank you."

She did not wait but the footman opened the door as she walked through it to where the carriage was waiting under the portico.

To his surprise she did not turn round to say any more, but merely stepped into the carriage.

Seeing how grand the house was the cabman had stepped down from his seat on the box. The Duke drew two guineas from the pocket of his robe.

"Take this lady to 27 Praed Street," he said. "You have been well paid, and you are not to demand any more from her than I have already given you."

The cabby looked at the money almost incredulously, then grinned.

"Thank ye, Sir! Oi 'opes for yer patronage anuvver night."

The way he spoke told the Duke that he thought he was taking home a prostitute who had amused a Gentleman of Fashion and might, if she was lucky, be invited back another evening.

For a moment there was a frown between the Duke's eyes at the impertinence of it. Then he realised it was the obvious explanation of his appearance and Vanola's destination.

He stepped back and the cabby, who had regained his seat on the box, whipped up his tired horse and the carriage drove off.

The Duke glanced at the window expecting Vanola to lean forward and wave to him as any other woman would have done, but there was no sign of her.

The carriage turned into Park Lane and he walked into the house and up the stairs while the footman closed the front door and bolted it.

As the Duke went into his Sitting-Room to blow out the lights he thought that what had occurred this evening had been so extraordinary that he could hardly believe it had happened.

Yet lying on the piano where he had not noticed them before were the compositions, which Vanola had played to him neatly copied out on music paper.

He knew when tomorrow he took them to the audition they would astound the other judges he had co-opted simply because he had thought they would save him a lot of extra work.

They were all men at the top of the profession and he knew that nothing they had heard so far could equal in any way the music that Sandor Szeleti had created.

As he picked them up he supposed it would have been reasonable for him to have asked Vanola to play them at the audition as she had played them for him tonight, and he wondered why he had not done so.

Then he knew that it was because he was reluctant not only that the judges should see her, but also those who had prevented her father's music from being entered for the Competition without first being bribed.

He intended to make a row about it which would vibrate through the whole music world, and did not wish her to be involved.

He felt it was because she had been through so much already, and because she appeared so frail and was on the verge of a breakdown owing to acute starvation, that he was concerned for her.

Then he was honest enough to admit that she was very beautiful and although he could not quite explain it, he wanted to keep her, for the moment at any rate, to himself.

'I am like a man,' he thought, 'who has found a perfect pearl in the depths of the sea and wishes to enjoy the beauty of it before proclaiming his find to the world in general.'

It was a wistful idea that made him smile, but when at length he went into his own room, got into bed, and lay in the darkness, he was thinking not about himself, as he had been doing before, but about Vanola.

chapter three

"His Grace isn't down yet, M'Lord," the Butler said as Lord Poolbrook came in through the front door.

'Brooky' as he was always known to his contemporaries, was one of the Duke's oldest friends, and his closest.

They had been at Eton together, gone on to Oxford in the same year, and served in the same Regiment.

But while the Duke was regarded with awe even by men of his own age, 'Brooky' was universally popular.

He was always cheerful, always prepared to make the best of any circumstances, and the Duke found him a companion he not only trusted with his closest secrets, but who was at times of more help than anyone else he knew.

Brooky was therefore included in everything the Duke did, whether it was on the race-course, or in the gay, amusing world in which, because Brooky was also a bachelor, he was almost as much in demand as the Duke himself.

Good-looking in a very English manner with fair hair, a sun-burnt complexion and eyes as blue as the sky, he handed his tall hat to the Butler saying as he did so:

"How is the rheumatism, Newman?"

"It's better, thank you, M'Lord. The warm weather always helps."

"That is what my mother says," Brooky replied, and walked towards the Dining Room.

When the Duke was in London, he almost invariably had breakfast with him, and as he himself lived in a flat in Half Moon Street with only a manservant to look after him, he appreciated the long row of silver dishes on the side-table in the Dining Room which contained, he knew, everything that any man could desire for breakfast.

The Butler and a footman brought in the coffee which they put on the table, then withdrew, leaving Lord Poolbrook alone until a moment later the Duke appeared.

He walked into the room and Brooky looked up from his plate to say:

"You must have been late last night to oversleep. I presume you were with some 'Fair Charmer,' otherwise I would have driven home with you."

The Duke did not reply, but there was an expression on his face which made Brooky ask:

"What has happened?"

"Why should you think anything has happened?" the Duke asked evasively, as he helped himself to the dishes on the side-table.

"You cannot deceive me," Brooky said. "You look different from the way you did yesterday, and definitely different from how you looked when you left Lady Lawson so early. She was biting her nails with fury at having failed in her plan to capture you as she had intended."

The Duke was not angry as he would have been if any other man had spoken about his personal affairs in such a way. He and Brooky were so closely attuned to each other that it was usually impossible for either of them to keep anything hidden from the other.

"Did you really expect me to stay behind last night?" he asked curiously.

"It was always an odds-on chance," Brooky replied. "After all, Eileen Lawson is very attractive and she has been panting after you quite obviously for the last month. In fact the betting in White's is that you will fall for her in the end."

The Duke scowled and Brooky said:

"Oh, stop being so pompous, Lenox. You know as well as I do that it is impossible to keep anything secret from those old gossip-mongers in White's and Boodles, and you are the most exciting person they have to talk about."

"I wish they would mind their own business!" the Duke said angrily.

"Of course you do," Brooky agreed, "but think how dull their lives would be without you."

The Duke laughed as if he could not help it. Then he said:

"You are coming with me to Covent Garden this morning?"

"If you want me to," Brooky replied. "I did think it would be more enjoyable to ride in the Row. I am sick of listening to that dreary music we heard yesterday, which would not evoke a whistle from an errand-boy."

"It will be very different this morning," the Duke promised.

"How do you know? I will bet you that Littleton, or whatever your Manager is called, sends the best of the bunch in first."

"He will send in the ones who have paid him the most," the Duke said.

His voice was so sharp and bitter that Brooky put down his knife and fork and looked across the table in astonishment.

"What are you saying?"

"I am saying that I have discovered something which has disgusted and infuriated me," the Duke replied, "and I need your support this morning because I am going to cause an almighty row that will shake the very foundations of the Opera House!"

Brooky sat back in his chair.

"Good!" he said. "Then I shall certainly come! It is a long time since I have seen you going into battle, and it is something which will undoubtedly do you good."

"I do not know what you mean by that."

"Then I will tell you," Brooky replied. "You have been getting into a rut, Lenox, and I have found it peculiarly depressing. Now, unless I am mistaken, something has woken you up, and nothing could be better timed than what you call 'an almighty row'!"

The Duke stared at his friend in amazement.

"I had no idea you felt like this about me. Why did you not tell me before?"

"What could I say?" Brooky asked. "You would not have been pleased to be told that you were growing pompous and too damned sure of yourself, and about as vital as the statue of you they will no doubt erect in the Park at Arkholme when you die."

The Duke put back his head and laughed.

"I have never heard you so eloquent."

"I have a great deal more to say on the subject, if you are interested," Brooky replied, "but now I want to hear what you have discovered, and why it has made you so angry."

The Duke drank some of his coffee before he began:

"When I woke up this morning I thought what had happened last night must have been a dream, so the first thing I did was to walk into my Sitting-Room and look at the piano to see if the music was there. It is so exceptional that I thought it could have existed only in my imagination."

He paused and Brooky leaning forward asked:

"What music? Whatever are you talking about?"

Slowly, choosing his words carefully, the Duke narrated in detail what had happened the night before.

Only when he had finished with Vanola driving away in a hackney carriage did Brooky exclaim:

"I do not believe it! It is more dramatic than anything I have ever seen in Drury Lane! Yet if it is true, it could only happen to you."

"Why only to me?" the Duke asked.

"Because you invite the unusual and always have," Brooky said. "Do you remember at Oxford..."

He stopped.

"Never mind. We can talk about that another time. What are you going to do, first about the corruption in your own particular province, and secondly about the girl?"

"I am going to sack Littleton," the Duke answered, "and anybody else who has taken money from a composer. Those who have already paid will have their money returned to them, and I somehow have to get in touch with those who were turned away."

"You intend that this corruption shall be reported to the newspapers?" Brooky asked.

"I would prefer not," the Duke answered. "At the same time, how else can I ensure that those who have lost hope of obtaining what Vanola called 'justice' will try again unless they realise they now will not have to pay for the privilege?"

"It is certainly going to be rather difficult," Brooky agreed. "I can hardly credit that Littleton, who seemed a quite decent sort of man, would stoop to behaving in such a disgraceful manner, considering the amount of money you have poured into Covent Garden."

"I suppose he thought he did not get enough of it for himself," the Duke replied.

There was a pause while both men went on eating their breakfast. Then Brooky said:

"Does this man Szeleti's music really sound as good as you say it is?"

"Better!" the Duke answered. "It is exactly what I have been looking for, a new Strauss, and a finer musician than he is, to present to the British public music which will raise their hearts and start them dancing."

Brooky laughed.

"I have always believed it would take an earthquake to do that, but if you are convinced, then those who like you are becoming pompous as they approach middle-age will undoubtedly be rejuvenated."

"One more word," the Duke said, "and I will not allow you to come with me, and you know you would not want to miss out on what I expect will be a very explosive morning."

"Nothing could keep me away," Brooky laughed. "If there is one thing I enjoy more than anything else, Lenox, it is when there is fire in your eyes and flames coming out of your mouth."

"You make me sound like a dragon!"

"That is exactly what you are when you are aroused. The trouble is that for the last few years you have been becoming more and more somnolent."

He paused, then added:

"However, now that I think about it, St. George has arrived in the shape of a lady called Vanola."

"And she was just as scathing as you! She condemned me for not being aware of what was going on, and practically accused me of inefficiency."

"Good for her!" Brooky exclaimed. "When I meet her I will congratulate her."

The Duke did not reply and after a moment Brooky said in a different tone of voice:

"What are you going to do about her father?"

The Duke paused for a moment before he said:

"I have already told Carstairs to take nourishing food made by my Chef and some wine to their lodgings in Praed Street as soon as possible. I have a feeling I can hardly ask Sir Felix Wrayton to attend a patient at that particular address."

"I can see his face if you did!" Brooky remarked.

"I therefore told Carstairs," the Duke went on, "to persuade Vanola to remove her father to a different address, and certainly to one that is not in the Borough of Paddington."

"You are right there," Brooky said. "The whole district is a disgrace. It ought to have been cleaned up years ago!"

"But, as she said, lodgings there are cheap," the Duke remarked.

"I presume you gave her some money?"

"Naturally. But she only accepted it on the condition that if her father won, as I assured her he would, the thousand guineas prize for the best composer, either I would deduct it, or she would return it to me immediately."

Brooky looked at the Duke incredulously.

"Did she really say that?"

"Most strongly, and I had the feeling that if she had not been so concerned about her father she would have refused to take even a penny from me."

"Good God! She is certainly unusual. I have never known a woman yet who did not have her hand in your pocket almost before you had asked her name!"

The Duke was about to say that this was untrue, when he remembered how much he had spent on the beautiful women who, while they loved him unrestrainedly, were always prepared to accept jewellery, furs and anything else which took their fancy.

Because he was so rich, they looked on it almost as their right, and he often thought that the women of his own class were more avaricious and more acquisitive than any mistress whose profession entitled her to extract as much as possible from her Protector.

"Did you say this girl was pretty?" Brooky asked.

"Beautiful is the right word," the Duke replied, "and she looks very Hungarian, except that her skin is almost dazzlingly white, which may be of course the result of starvation."

"She sounds unusual."

"She is," the Duke agreed. "I went outside this morning to look at where she had climbed up the side of the house. She must also have climbed over the wall from the Mews, because the door is always kept locked."

"I should have thought it was quite a job even for an experienced Burglar to enter the house in such a way," Brooky observed.

"I thought the same," the Duke agreed, "and a man would have found it difficult to obtain a foothold on the wisteria which would not have taken the weight of anybody heavy. But Vanola is extremely light."

"Due to starvation, of course."

"Exactly!" the Duke agreed. "I expect she will find it hard to eat even a little of the food I have ordered for them. I have always been told that one gets to a stage where having eaten very little for so long, one is no longer hungry."

"I have seen children like that abroad," Brooky agreed, "and even though they begged for food, when one gave it to them it seemed impossible for them to swallow it."

The Duke was thinking how hard it had been to persuade Vanola to eat the pâté sandwiches and remembered in fact that it was only because he had made her drink the champagne that she had been able to force them down her throat.

Without saying so aloud he made up his mind that as soon as he had finished the difficulties of Covent

Garden, he would go himself to Praed Street, if Carstairs had not persuaded her to leave, and insist on her doing so.

"By the time I have finished bringing Sandor Szeleti's music to the world," he said aloud, "he will be a very rich man!"

"Then it is certainly imperative that he should not die before that happens," Brooky replied.

The Duke looked at him in a startled fashion as if it had not occurred to him before.

"You are right!" he said. "I will tell Carstairs whatever the conditions in which they are living, to find a doctor who will attend him. There must be dozens in the neighbourhood who would be only too pleased to know they can send the bill to me."

"They will be delighted!" Brooky agreed. "But they will certainly think it strange that with your unlimited choice you should have a Lady-friend living in Praed Street!"

For a moment the Duke scowled then realised he was teasing and laughed.

"If you suggested such a thing to Vanola she would doubtless fire at you with her pistol," he said. "She did not consider me as a man, but as a Patron of Music, who had failed miserably to live up to his pretentions."

Brooky laughed.

"Poor Lenox! It must be the first time that your audience, which is a very large one, has booed instead of giving you a standing ovation!"

"If what Vanola says is true, and musicians have been turned away because they could not pay the fee that was illegally demanded of them, then I suppose

I am to blame for being unaware of what was going on."

"You do not suppose this girl was lying in order to evoke your sympathy?" Brooky suggested.

The Duke shook his head.

"No, she was telling the truth, there is no doubt about that."

He rose from the table saying:

"Come on, Brooky, let us be on our way to Covent Garden where I intend to raise the roof!"

* * *

It was late in the afternoon when the Duke and Brooky drove back to Park Lane.

When the Duke had said he would raise the roof he had certainly meant it, and in the row that ensued not only Littleton was dismissed from his post, but several other men in subordinate positions left the Royal Opera House for the last time.

The Judges, like the Duke, expressed horror when they learned what had happened, although Brooky had a faint suspicion that one or two of them at any rate had an idea of what was going on.

But one thing was very certain—they could not afford to lose the Duke's patronage, and had no wish personally to antagonize him in any way.

They therefore agreed heartily to anything he suggested and the way he reprimanded Littleton and those who had collaborated with him left the men white and shaking before they finally walked out of the building jobless and with no employer's reference.

Brooky watched with admiration the way the Duke

handled the whole situation.

He never raised his voice, but the way he spoke made every word sound like the crack of a whip, and when finally the Manager left the room both Brooky and the other Judges seemed to sigh deeply as if to relieve the tension which all the time the Duke was speaking had kept them rigid.

Not until that matter had been settled had the Duke gone into the room where the Competitors who had come for the audition were waiting apprehensively.

They were aware that something was going on, and were afraid that whatever it was might prevent them from getting a hearing.

The Duke talked to them, discovered exactly what money had been extorted from each of them, and arranged that they should be repaid immediately.

He then asked them if they had any idea of the names of those who had been turned away because they could not afford to pay for the privilege of being auditioned.

He was disappointed to find that out of twenty men waiting for him they knew the names of only two other applicants.

All the time he was listening during the rest of the morning to those who played their compositions on the stage while he and the other Judges sat in the Stalls, he was wondering how he could get in touch with those who had left in despair.

He could not help thinking that they might be suffering as Sandor Szeleti and his daughter were, and he found his mind wandering when he should have been listening.

Once or twice he left a decision to the other Judges,

rather than as was more usual, giving his own opinion with which they concurred.

By one o'clock they were all growing somewhat tired, and the Duke and Brooky drove from Covent Garden to White's, for a quick luncheon before they returned for more auditions in the afternoon.

He had left implicit instructions that if anybody should come to the door they should be welcomed and invited to join those who were already there.

Then as they drove away Brooky said:

"The only performance I think was really outstanding this morning was yours!"

"There is certainly no doubt those men were guilty," the Duke replied.

"I wonder how much they have accumulated over the years," Brooky said ruminatively. "They must have extorted money on many other occasions as well as this."

The Duke remembered what Vanola had said about the Concert he had arranged in aid of the Children's Hospital. Sandor Szeleti had come to England especially for it, but his inability to find engagements as a violinist, had ruined his health and, if Vanola was to be believed, killed his wife.

"Money undoubtedly corrupts," he said bitterly.

"Only if one does not have enough of it," Brooky replied.

"I suppose that is true," the Duke said, "but does anybody ever have enough? It is like some insidious drug; the more you have, the more you want, and I have never yet met a man who was satisfied with his lot."

"Except you," Brooky said. "I have never known

you yet, Lenox, to say that there was something you really wanted, but could not afford."

"What I want cannot be bought with money," the Duke replied.

"What is that?"

The Duke did not answer. He was thinking he had made a mistake in saying that, thinking that not even to Brooky could he confess that last night he had been introspective enough to ask himself what he wanted of life.

He knew that somehow he was disappointed and frustrated but why he had no idea.

Brooky was aware he had no wish to say any more and they drove on in silence. Only when they reached White's and were hailed effusively by a number of the Duke's friends did they talk of other things.

Back at Covent Garden the Composers followed each other rather monotonously. At the end of the day there were just two who seemed worthwhile. The Duke kept their compositions and he was determined they should receive enough money to keep them in comfort while they tried to get engagements.

Then as a finale he called an accompanist to the piano to play the works of Sandor Szeleti.

As some of the compositions that were brought to the audition were for the violin or cello, rather than the piano, the Duke always had an accompanist in attendance whom he considered to be one of the finest in London.

Now as the man sat down at the piano the Duke handed him the music which Vanola had left him the night before, and he said as he looked at it:

"This is rather different from what we have heard so far, Your Grace."

"I thought you would think that," the Duke replied, "and I am sure the other gentlemen here will agree."

When the accompanist had finished playing the three compositions there was a silence that was more eloquent than words.

Then simultaneously they all started to clap with an enthusiasm which had not animated them before.

"Wonderful!" "Magnificent!" "Superb!"

The adjectives flew from their lips, and the Duke said:

"I think, gentlemen, we need not look any further for the winner of this Competition. What you have to decide, and I am quite prepared to leave it in your hands, is who are to have the other prizes."

The other Composers whom the Duke had chosen were made extremely happy to learn that they were to divide the second prize of five hundred guineas between them, and others who were really nonentities were awarded £100 each.

'It will keep them from starving,' the Duke thought, 'although it is difficult to believe they will be able to live for any length of time on their own work.'

That still left the problem of those who had been turned away, and he therefore asked to meet several newspaper reporters who had been waiting to hear the results of the Competition.

In somewhat guarded language he told them that he understood there had been some mistake over the arrangements relating to the audition.

He wished them to make it clear that there would be another Competition for which he was prepared to offer the same prizes, and that everybody who entered it would be seen personally, not at Covent Garden, but in his Music Room at Park Lane in two weeks time.

As this was something which had never happened before he knew his decision would get wide coverage, and the reporters hurried away far more interested in the audition that was to come than the one which had just taken place.

At the same time, the Duke had made it very clear to them that the winner, Sandor Szeleti, was in his opinion a hitherto unappreciated genius, although he was known as a violinist in his own country.

"I think, gentlemen," he concluded, "we have discovered a Composer who will shine like a new light in the Music World, and whose melodies will in a very short time be on everyone's lips, and singing in everybody's ears."

He thought as he spoke that it was the sort of phrase that would please Vanola, and he thought it would have been amusing to see her face tomorrow morning when she read the newspapers.

Then he remembered it would be unlikely she would be able to afford to buy them, and that was something else he would have to send round to Praed Street, or wherever Mr. Carstairs had persuaded them to move to.

As he and Brooky drove back to Park Lane, the latter said:

"All I can tell you is that after all that I need a very strong drink! What are you doing this evening?"

"I cannot remember," the Duke replied.

"I believe you are dining at Richmond House," Brooky said. "I accepted a week ago, and I am sure you did too."

The Duke groaned.

"I feel almost too tired to make the effort to amuse the Duchess this evening."

Brooky laughed.

"Shall we send a note to say that we are unfortunately detained?" the Duke suggested.

"You must be crazy!" Brooky replied. "That is the sort of slight the Duchess never forgets, nor forgives."

"Then of course we must go."

"A bottle of your best champagne is undoubtedly the tonic we both need at the moment."

"Very well," the Duke agreed, "but I do not intend to stay for long."

"You will doubtless change your mind once you get there," Brooky said cheerfully. "One thing about the Richmonds is they invite all the most beautiful women in London to their parties."

"I suppose that is true," the Duke said indifferently.

"I was thinking when we were there last," Brooky went on, "that somebody ought to paint a picture of us all dancing under the chandeliers. I thought the women looked so graceful in their crinolines. That reminds me, your musical friend could not have climbed into your house if she had worn a crinoline."

"That is certainly true," the Duke agreed. "But wearing one she could have easily graced a ball at Richmond House."

Brooky glanced at him and said:

"You should invite her to dance with you sometime."

"If I did," the Duke replied, "she would certainly refuse. I have told you she despises me and her voice vibrates full of contempt."

Brooky contemplated saying such unusual behaviour was good for him after so much adulation. But before he could speak the carriage drew up outside Arkholme House.

The Duke walked into the Hall.

"Where is the champagne, Newman?" he asked.

"In the Library, Your Grace," the Butler replied. "Is there anything else Your Grace requires?"

"I am hungry," Brooky said. "You hurried us so over luncheon that I feel now I shall starve if I do not have something to eat before dinner."

The Duke nearly said that Brooky did not know the meaning of the word, then thought it would be a mistake. Instead he sent the Butler hurrying for sandwiches, knowing that if he was at home at the right time the Chef was always prepared to provide him with a very large English tea.

As they walked towards the Study the Duke said:

"Send Mr. Carstairs to me."

"Very good, Your Grace."

They had only been in the Study for a few minutes before the Duke's secretary appeared. A tall man, whose hair was turning grey and who looked perpetually worried came quietly into the room.

"Well, Carstairs?" the Duke said. "Did you persuade Miss Szeleti and her father to move to a more savoury neighbourhood than Paddington?"

"I am afraid not, Your Grace."

"Why not?"

"Because, Your Grace, when I arrived at 27 Praed Street, Miss Szeleti and her father had already left."

The Duke stared at his secretary incredulously. Then he said sharply:

"What time did you get there?"

"It was after 3:30 P.M. Your Grace, as Chef had some trouble procuring the right ingredients he required for his dishes for an ill man."

"Did you enquire whether they had left an address?"

"Of course, Your Grace, but nobody in the house had the slightest idea where they had gone."

The way Mr. Carstairs spoke told the Duke without words that the inhabitants of the house were determined to divulge no information in case it should be used against them.

To ask questions of women of a certain profession always aroused suspicions that the questioner might come from the police.

"But somebody," the Duke persisted, "must have been aware that they had left, and I presume they paid for their lodging?"

"Yes, indeed, Your Grace, I spoke to the proprietress of the building, a slovenly woman who was in the kitchen."

"What did she say?"

"She said that Miss Szeleti, although she could not pronounce the name correctly, had paid all she owed, and taken her father away in a hackney carriage. He had been carried downstairs by the cab-driver and another man who had given him a hand. That was all she knew."

The Duke was silent, and Brooky said:

"They had obviously gone to better lodgings. Do not worry, Lenox, they will get in touch with you when the announcement that Sandor Szeleti has won the award appears in tomorrow's newspapers."

"Yes, of course," the Duke agreed.

At the same time he had a strange, unaccountable feeling that he had lost something very precious.

* * *

69

Vanola had moved her father back to the lodgings where they had stayed when her mother was alive.

They were in a much better class of street than Praed Street and when she called to see their former landlady, a Mrs. Bates, the woman had been delighted to see her.

"I've often thought about you, me dear," she said, "and how sad it was losing your pretty mother the way you did. I'd only to look at her to say to myself . . . that's a lady, that is . . . and I'm never mistaken."

"Thank you," Vanola replied, "but you will understand, Mrs. Bates, that Papa is very ill indeed, and I must move him to where he can be more comfortable and will have a chance of recovering."

Before Mrs. Bates could reply she said:

"I can pay for the best room you have, in advance."

"It's just a bit of luck," Mrs. Bates answered, "that the nicest room in the house has just become vacant. Ever such a pleasant gentleman's been in it this last fortnight, but he's had to go North, and I doubt if he'll be South again for several months."

When Vanola saw the room she knew that while it was sparsely furnished and by no means particularly comfortable, it was in every way much better than the sordid, rat-infested attic in Praed Street.

There was a bow-window which faced South, and although the bed was small and rather rickety, there was a carpet of sorts on the floor and a tiny room through a communicating door where she could sleep.

There was not the comfort of the place in which they had stayed when they had first come to London, and nothing like the apartment they had occupied in Paris.

70

But at least it was comparatively clean, and she was aware that Mrs. Bates was particular whom she took as lodgers.

She would not tolerate what she described as 'them dirty goings-on' in her house.

But actually, although Vanola knew it would have shocked her mother, the prostitutes in Praed Street had been kind in their own way once they realised she had an ill man on her hands and was in no way a competitor of theirs.

They would ask her about her father and tell her in their own manner to cheer up, and that there was always 'a rainbow round the corner,' which was something which until Vanola had decided to challenge the Duke she had believed was a fallacy.

When she finally got her father back into Mrs. Bates's lodging-house and into bed, she had insisted on his drinking the soup she made in the kitchen downstairs from a very good piece of beef which she had bought as soon as the shops opened first thing in the morning.

She had known he had to be nourished, and although he drank a little milk to please her before they changed their lodgings, she had not dared to cook anything in the filthy, cockroach-ridden kitchen in which their landlady in Praed Street sat drinking gin until she was too drunk to even keep the fire alight.

When Vanola looked at her father he appeared so pale and white leaning back against the pillows on the bed, that she felt a constriction of her heart because she feared that he had stopped breathing.

Then he moved and she sat down hurriedly beside him to feed him the soup.

"It is a good soup, Papa, made with best beef, and

you will soon feel your strength coming back to you."

She had already told him that his composition had won the first prize in the Competition arranged at Covent Garden by the Duke of Arkholme, but she had the feeling that he did not understand what she was saying.

In fact, when he woke up that morning, he had thought that she was her mother.

"I know you are—ill, Melina—my darling," he said, "and I am—worried as to what—will happen to—us."

"It is going to be all right, now, Papa," Vanola replied, "and listen to me: I am Vanola, not Mama."

Her father had opened his eyes and she thought they seemed glazed, as if they saw not reality but the world in which he had been dreaming.

Even though he looked so ill he was still undeniably handsome.

Although his hair was beginning to turn grey, it was still thick and brushed back from his square forehead, and it made him look very distinguished and at the same time very Hungarian.

"Listen to me, Papa," she repeated. "You have won a great deal of money with your compositions, and the Duke of Arkholme thinks you are a genius."

Her father closed his eyes and she knew it was hopeless.

When she had persuaded him to drink a little milk before he went to sleep she knew that the weeks of starvation, when they had existed on little more than bread of the coarsest kind and food which often smelt suspiciously unpleasant, had left him without the will to live.

When Vanola had hired a carriage to take them to

their new lodgings she asked the cab-driver who seemed a kindly man if he would go to the Tavern on the corner and buy a small bottle of brandy.

As soon as he understood why she needed it, he brought it back quickly, and with the help of another man who apparently had nothing better to do, they carried Sandor Szeleti downstairs and placed him in the hackney carriage.

Vanola had changed one of the sovereigns which the Duke had given her when she had bought the milk and when she had given the cab-driver and the other man who had helped her father a shilling each for their pains, they had looked at her doubtfully.

"Sure ye can afford it, Miss?" the cab-driver had asked. "Ye've got a very sick man there."

"I know that," Vanola replied, "but I have a little money to tide us over until Papa is better. Then he will be able to earn some with his music."

"Musical, be 'e?" the cab-driver asked. "Oi've never known one o' 'em to ride round with a fur rug over 'is knees."

He laughed at his own joke. Then Vanola said:

"Thank you for being so kind and helping us. It is a pity there are not more people in the world like you."

"It's bin a pleasure, an' ye get yerself someat' to eat an' put a bit o' colour in yer cheeks," the cab-driver advised.

Vanola smiled at him as he drove off, then ran back to be with her father.

The nourishing soup and the brandy she made him drink certainly seemed to revive him a little, and he began to talk more sensibly.

"Did you say—the Duke of Arkholme—liked my

73

music?" he asked. "Or—did I—imagine it?"

"He said you were a genius, Papa, and that you will receive the thousand guineas he has offered for the best composition he hears."

For a moment there seemed to be a new light in Sandor Szeleti's eyes, but then he said in a voice his daughter could hardly hear:

"It is—too late—I cannot—play now for your—mother."

chapter four

DURING the afternoon Sandor Szeleti seemed to grow worse. When he did speak his words were rambling and he was talking most of the time as if to his wife.

Although Vanola kept feeding him with the beef soup which she heated up continually in Mrs. Bates's kitchen, she began to feel afraid.

Finally she said to Mrs. Bates:

"I must fetch the doctor to Papa. Is that nice Dr. Urban who attended my mother when she died still practising?"

"I thinks so," Mrs. Bates replied, "but I've not seen him lately. I tell you what, I'll tell Billy to pop round to his house—it's not far—and ask him to call and see you."

"I should be very grateful if Billy could do that," Vanola said.

She then ran upstairs to her father's bedside thinking that she should have sent for the doctor before now, but she had never had enough money to pay him, even though Dr. Urban was very much cheaper than any other doctor she knew.

This was because, although he was not Hungarian, he was an Austrian. Her mother and father had both liked him and found him in many ways a congenial companion.

In fact, for the few shillings the doctor charged when he visited them, Vanola thought he spent considerably more time at her mother's bedside than he did with his more wealthy patients.

When she reached the bedroom her father was quieter than he had been before, but was still mumbling a little beneath his breath.

She thought perhaps he had a fever, but when she put her hand on his forehead it was cold. At the same time he was sweating and he looked so desperately pale that she was afraid.

She thought it was rather the way her mother had looked before she died quite quietly without saying anything to them. It was as if her spirit had slipped out of her body and they were left with nothing but an empty shell.

Valona sat down beside her father and took his cold hand in hers.

She was willing him to stay alive, and she felt as if the intensity of her feelings must communicate itself to him.

They had always been so close and after her mother had died she knew her father clung to her and she was the one thing in his life apart from his music that brought him any happiness.

"I must not let you go, Papa," she said silently. "You have won the Competition and now everything will be different. We will find a comfortable place to live, and I am sure if you are well fed and kept warm you will soon be able to play your violin again."

Even if he could not do that, she thought, if the Duke was to be believed, his music would make him a lot of money and bring him the fame that had eluded him since he left his own country.

That in itself, Vanola knew, would bring him a sense of satisfaction, and she was quite certain that if he was encouraged his ability to compose would develop and he would write down still more of the melodies he had played for so long, and which came from his imagination, or rather, Vanola thought, from his very soul.

"There are so many things we can do together, now that we can afford it," she said aloud, thinking perhaps her voice would reach him and she could give him the will to live.

"We can go to Operas and Concerts," she went on, "and once you are well known it will be like it was at home when Mama told me how the best seats in the House were always at your disposal, or even the Royal Box, if it was not being occupied for that performance."

As she spoke she had a vision of her father looking extremely handsome and very smart in his evening-clothes, and with herself wearing instead of the threadbare rags she had on now, a fashionable gown with a velvet wrap trimmed with fur around her shoulders.

Sometimes she and her mother had pretended they

were going to the Opera in Paris, and to a Reception afterwards in one of the grand houses in the Champs Élysées.

They had described their gowns and the fans they would carry, and the flowers that were sent by her father's admirers from which they could select a nosegay to wear pinned at their breasts or in their hair.

They would choose the menu, with dishes to tempt the appetite before the Opera commenced, and what would be served at supper afterwards.

They would laugh at their own imaginations and yet Vanola could see it happening in pictures as if she was watching herself upon a stage.

"Perhaps the Duke will ask us to dine with him at his house in Park Lane, where he has a Music Room, Papa," she said aloud, "and he will give a Concert afterwards in which you will play to the most famous music lovers in England. Also I know the Queen would enjoy your Hungarian folk-songs, which are gayer and more lively than anything Offenbach has ever written."

She thought because she was talking in a low, distinct tone that her father must be listening. Then suddenly she felt his fingers tighten on hers and he opened his eyes.

Before she could rise to assist him he sat up.

"Be careful, Papa!" she warned.

Then she saw that her father was not looking at her, but at something he saw at the end of the bed and there was a light in his eyes that had not been there for a long time.

"Melina!" he exclaimed, and his voice suddenly sounded young, strong and excited. "Oh, my darling, I have missed you more than I can say!"

Then, as he spoke and Vanola knew he was seeing her mother, he collapsed backwards against the pillows.

* * *

The Duke walked into the Library and found Brooky reading the newspapers.

He looked around with a smile on his face and when he saw the expression on the Duke's he rose to his feet saying:

"I suppose there is no news?"

"None at all," the Duke replied.

"I have just been reading your announcement in both the *Times* and the *Morning Post*," Brooky said. "Surely if the girl does not see it herself there must be people in the same house, or friends who will read it and tell her what it says."

"I would think so," the Duke said dryly. "But I have the feeling that her father must have died."

"Why should you think that?" Brooky asked.

The Duke did not reply, but he was thinking of how Vanola had said that it might be too late to help her father.

He was also remembering the condemnation in her voice when she told him how everything had gone wrong since they had come to England and her father could not play in the Concert he had arranged.

Although it seemed incredible, he had lain awake for the last three nights fighting against the idea that Vanola blamed him not only for her father's failure to gain recognition in England, but also for her mother's death.

"If they do not turn up," Brooky asked, "what are

you going to do with the money?"

"Do not be so ridiculous!" the Duke replied sharply. "Two people cannot disappear completely, especially if it is a question of their receiving a large sum of money."

Brooky knew he had annoyed the Duke, and therefore said in a more conciliatory tone:

"I agree with you, it must be possible to find them. If Sandor Szeleti is as ill as you say, she could not take him very far, so I imagine they will still be somewhere in the Paddington district."

"Yes, of course," the Duke agreed, "and she did say they had been in better lodgings before her mother died."

"Then send somebody round to all the most likely lodgings in that area," Brooky suggested.

"I have thought of that already," the Duke replied, "and Carstairs has, I believe, engaged several ex-Policemen to see what they can find out."

Brooky did not answer, but he raised his eyebrows, realising that the Duke was certainly taking the hunt for the girl very seriously.

In fact, he had never known him to concentrate on anything so intensely as he was doing now in what he thought of as 'the hunt for Vanola.'

It seemed extraordinary that after the girl had taken the trouble to climb into the Duke's private Sitting-Room and force him to listen to her at gunpoint, she should then disappear and be content with £50 when there was a further thousand guineas waiting for collection.

What was more, as the Duke had told Brooky last night, he had already given Sandor Szeleti's music to the Publishers and the sheets were being run off on the Presses and would be in the Music Shops and on the streets tomorrow.

As he thought of it he said:

"One thing is certain: if Vanola does not see the newspapers, the moment the music is being played and sung she will certainly recognise her father's tunes, even if they are only whistled by an errand-boy."

"That is what I am telling myself will happen," the Duke replied, but he did not sound very optimistic about it.

"What about the other Competitors? Did they have no luck with their compositions?"

"I believe there is a Publisher who is interested in the two Composers who tied for second place," the Duke said, "but the fact that they are under my patronage and I have allowed them to use my name on the cover of the music, is what they are keen on promoting."

The Duke sat down at his desk and after a moment drummed with his fingers on it, in a way which meant he was extremely irritated.

He was usually a very controlled person, and Brooky was aware that he was not only restless but showing signs of frustration that made him very different from what he had been before Vanola came into his life.

"It is one thing to give him a new interest,' Brooky thought, 'but quite another to take it away just when she had aroused him in a way I find strange and completely unpredictable.'

He was, however, too wise to say this aloud, and he merely rose and walked towards the grog-tray saying:

"Can I help you to a drink?"

The Duke did not reply, but was staring ahead. Brooky had the idea that he was looking back into the past, trying to find some clue which would solve the complicated puzzle of Vanola.

The door opened and a servant came into the room with a note on a silver salver.

He held it out to the Duke who took it without much interest.

"This was left for Your Grace," the footman said, "at the front door by a ragged boy who said it was important it should be given to Your Grace personally and to nobody else."

The Duke started and sat upright.

"A ragged boy?" he questioned.

"Yes, Your Grace, and those were 'is very words, Your Grace, so I thinks I should do as 'e asked."

"Quite right," the Duke answered.

He picked up the note and was staring at it as the servant left the room.

"What is it? Who is it from?" Brooky enquired.

The Duke did not answer, and Brooky knew by the expression on his face that it was what he had been waiting for.

Quickly he slit open the envelope, then as he turned it upside-down, several banknotes and two soverigns fell out onto the Duke's gold-cornered leather blotter.

As Brooky walked to the desk to stand staring down at the money the Duke was searching the envelope and he drew out a small piece of paper on which were two words.

He sat looking at them as if he could hardly credit what he read, then without speaking he passed the piece of paper to Brooky.

In an educated hand in the centre of the piece of paper were inscribed just two words:

"Too late!"

"What does that mean?" Brooky asked.

"I should have thought that was obvious," the Duke replied. "Her father is dead and she has returned what is left of the £50 I gave her."

He counted her money.

"Twenty-seven pounds, to be exact."

"I do not believe it," Brooky said. "How can she do such a thing?"

There was silence for a moment. Then the Duke said very slowly:

"She could only do it if having paid for her father's funeral, she has found employment of some sort."

He rose from his desk and walked across the room to the fireplace as if he could not be inactive. Then he said with his back to his friend:

"I have the strange feeling that the rest of the £50 will be returned to me, bit by bit, until she has cleared her debt."

"Why in the name of goodness should she do that?" Brooky asked. "After all, she must be aware that the money for her father's award is now hers."

"What is very clear to me," the Duke replied, "is that she is determined to accept no money, not even a penny, from me."

"Why should she feel like that?"

"Because she holds me responsible for her father's death, and also her mother's!"

"It is incredible! She must be hysterical!"

"No—proud!" the Duke corrected.

There was silence. Then he said almost as if he was speaking to himself:

"The only way she could earn money is by playing the piano. That is what we have to look for now: a place where she could play and perhaps teach. I have no idea what kind of place it could be, but I am sure it will somehow be connected with music."

* * *

Although the doctor had arrived too late to save Sandor Szeleti's life he had nevertheless been of inestimable help to Vanola.

"Why did you not send for me sooner?" he asked sharply when he saw how emaciated her father was.

"I . . . I did not know how to . . . pay you," Vanola replied, "and you have been so kind . . . already when . . . Mama died."

"How can you be so foolish?" the doctor asked. "I admired your father and thought he was one of the most interesting men I had ever met in my life. If you had asked me to attend him I would have gladly done so."

"Thank you," Vanola said quietly, "but it is too late now, and as I know he is with Mama . . . I think it will make him happy as he has not been for a long time."

She knew as she spoke she would never forget the thrill in her father's voice, and the way he suddenly spoke as if he was a young and ardent man because he had seen her mother again.

"That is love," she said to herself. "That is the true happiness which does not depend on money or success, but on two hearts being joined as one."

She knew that was what she would work to have in her own life, but thought it was exceedingly unlikely.

Looking back she knew with all their difficulties and privations her father had only borne them bravely, but at times because her mother was there, and they were together, they found them amusing.

"We should have stayed in Hungary," she told herself as she had done so many times before. "What was the gain if Papa was applauded by a lot of strangers? That he and Mama were so happy in their love for one another was far more important than anything else."

Dr. Urban arranged everything as regards the funeral, and because Mrs. Bates was anxious that nobody in the house should realise that a lodger had died, it took place very quickly.

"Death's always upsetting," she said, "and what's more, people don't like renting a room where someone's died. They think it might be haunted."

"I am sorry, Mrs. Bates. I should not have come to you," Vanola said.

"It's what you should have done before your father got so bad as he was," Mrs. Bates said. "But two deaths in the house don't do my reputation any good, and I trust you not to talk about it to any of the lodgers. I know the doctor'll hold his tongue."

"How could I do anything to hurt you after you have been so kind?" Vanola asked. "But please, could I stay in the little room until I can find work of some sort?"

"What do you think you can do to earn money?" Mrs. Bates asked.

Vanola did not reply, but she knew it was going to be very difficult. As her father's coffin was lowered into the grave she prayed not for him, knowing he was now happy with her mother, but for herself.

"Help me, Papa, help me!" she said in her heart.

Almost as if her prayers were answered, as she walked back from the Churchyard she met one of the women who had been lodging in Praed Street, and remembered her name was Evie.

She was just starting out on her evening patrol, her face gaudily painted, a bonnet trimmed with red feathers on top of her dyed hair.

"Hallo, dearie," she said as they met on the pavement. "Where have you bin? I heard as how you'd left."

"We moved to some other lodgings," Vanola replied. "Then my father...died and...I have just ...come from his...funeral."

"I'm ever so sorry, reelly I am!" Evie answered. "I always say hearin' of a death brings bad luck, an' that means I might as well go 'ome."

"Forgive me if I have upset you."

"It's not your fault, dearie," Evie said. "But wot are you goin' to do now that your Pa's dead?"

"I have to find work of some sort."

"That shouldn't be too difficult being as pretty as you are!"

Vanola did not reply and after a moment Evie added:

"But you're a Lidy. I can see that. Still, when you're reely on your uppers, I don't see much alternative to my way of life."

"The only thing I can do well," Vanola said as if she was following her own thoughts, "is play the piano."

86

"I heard as how your father was a musicaian, but I don't suppose you've got much chance of going on the stage."

"I would not want to do that," Vanola replied. "But perhaps I could be a teacher or play the piano for a Dancing Class."

Evie stared at her.

"Now that's an idea!" she said. "I thinks there's a job going, 'though they might not think you right for it, at Kate Hamilton's."

Vanola's eyes seemed to light up.

"Who is she?" she enquired.

"You mean you've never heard of Kate?"

"No, never."

"Oh, no, I suppose you wouldn't have, seein' as I says, that you're a Lidy."

"I do not think being a lady makes any difference when one is hungry."

Evie laughed.

"No, I s'pose not. A tummy's a tummy, whoever owns it. And if it's empty it can be damned uncomfortable!"

Vanola tried not to start as Evie swore, but asked:

"Where is this place? Can you tell me about it?"

"It may be filled by now, but one of the girls who moved out this morning to better lodgings because she's been taken on by Kate said as how there was a big bust-up there last night because the man wot plays the piano got drunk and Kate chucked him out. She had to put one of the girls to play the piano in his place, and that made her furious."

"Why should she be furious?" Vanola asked.

"Because it stopped her from enjoying herself with

the gentlemen, and that cost her money. D'you understand?"

Vanola had not the least idea what Evie was talking about, but after a moment she said tentatively:

"Do you think I would have a chance if I applied for the position?"

"You can do but, if you asks me, Kate'll offer you somethin' different an' I expect you'd enjoy the dancing!"

The way she spoke made Vanola think there was something wrong about the dancers and anyhow she had no wish to do anything but play for her living.

"Would you be very kind and give me the address of this Miss, or is it Mrs. Hamilton?"

"You'll have to be formal and call her 'Ma'am' if you're employed by her."

"Do you know the address?" Vanola asked.

"Prince's Street, off Leicester Square. It don't open for the gentry until nine o'clock in the evening, but if you hurries along there now you might be able to see Kate afore she gets busy."

Vanola hesitated a moment, then made up her mind.

She had no wish to return to her lodgings to cry for her father now she was alone. Besides, she was determined to earn her own living and pay back every penny she owed the Duke.

As the Duke had anticipated she had not seen the announcement in the newspapers that her father had won the prize, but Dr. Urban had not missed it.

"Strangely enough," he said to Vanola, "I was reading about your father this morning before I got your message."

"Reading about him?"

Dr. Urban looked at Vanola in surprise before he replied:

"You must be aware that he has won the thousand guineas offered by the Duke of Arkholme for the best composition in the Competition he has been holding at Covent Garden?"

"So it is in the newspapers!" Vanola said in a low voice.

"It certainly is," the Doctor said. "I would have brought a copy with me if I had suspected you had not seen it."

"It is too late now . . . much too late," Vanola answered.

* * *

Riding to Leicester Square in a hackney carriage which she thought was a vast extravagance, Vanola told herself she hated the Duke with a violence that made her want to throw her defiance in his face and tell him how despicable she thought he was.

"How dare he allow such trickery to go on without being aware of it?" she asked. "How dare he allow the men who turned my father away from the Concert for which he had come specially to England to fatten themselves on their ill-gotten gains and then plead ignorance?

"He should have investigated the whole proceedings," she went on in her mind. "He should have been intuitively aware that unscrupulous people would defame music by sucking the life-blood out of those who have given their lives for it. How could he have been so ignorant . . . so blind . . . so obtuse?"

She wished now that when she had the opportunity she had raged at him and told him exactly what she thought of him and how utterly comtemptible he was.

What had made her abstain was the fear that if she was too violent in her condemnation he would have had her thrown out of his house and she would have had no means of saving her father from dying of starvation.

She had obtained the money, but the words that kept repeating themselves over and over again in her brain were "Too late!"

'I will pay him back every penny!' she thought. 'Then I can forget him for ever.'

At the same time, she thought of how much the funeral had cost and however firmly the doctor tried to refuse the fee she had offered to him she had insisted on his taking it.

When she reached Kate Hamilton's establishment in Prince's Street, the door was opened by a young man in his shirt-sleeves.

"Yer too early!" he said, "and Kate ain't seein' anyone at this hour!"

"I have come about the situation as pianist," Vanola said quickly.

The words made the man pause before he closed the door.

"Pianist?" he asked. "Is that wot yer are?"

"Yes, and a very good one," Vanola replied.

He opened the door a little wider.

"Kate's looking for a man. 'Er don't like women playin' the piano."

"I can play better than most men."

He looked at her as if he thought she was lying. Then he said:

"If yer 'avin' me on, it'll be the worse for yer! I tells yer, Kate don't want no more gals at the moment. She's got enough of 'em and to spare."

"I am only interested in your piano," Vanola insisted.

He opened the door wide enough for her to pass in through it, and she walked into a long, tunnel-like passage at the end of which was a short flight of stairs.

It was lit artificially, at the moment by only one gas-lamp, and it looked strange and rather gloomy.

The man who had let her in was strong and muscular, but his hair was untidy, and he had not shaved.

"Now yer wait 'ere," he said, "and' I'll go and see wot Kate 'as to say about this. But if yer asks me, yer're wastin' your time."

He did not wait for Vanola to reply but walked up the stairs and opened a door. He shut it behind him and she was alone.

There were one or two rather gaudy-looking chairs painted in gold and with red velvet seats, and because she felt exhausted not only physically but also mentally after the strain of her father's funeral, she sat down on the edge of one and wondered if she was, as the man had said, wasting her time.

If it was a question just of playing the piano, she knew it would present no difficulty.

She had played ever since she had been small enough to stretch her fingers over the keys, and once she heard a tune she could play it from memory. Although she was a little shy about it, she could compose in the same way that her father could.

It seemed to Vanola that she waited for a long time, then the door at the top of the stairs opened and the man appeared.

"Come on," he said. "Kate'll see yer, and Gawd help yer if yer're lying!"

Vanola rose and walked up the stairs to find herself in a large Saloon.

Here too there was only one light to illuminate it, but she could see there was what looked like a counter, with a looking-glass behind it and a mass of bottles and glasses in front of it, and she thought it was what was called a 'Bar.'

At the other end of the room was a platform with a velvet chair on it. It looked as if it might be a stage on which there could be a performance of some sort.

She had not much time to notice anything else except the number of mirrors which covered the walls and which reflected and re-reflected her as she walked quickly down the room behind the man in his shirt-sleeves.

He opened another door and she saw there was a staircase and doors half-open which led into small rooms in which there appeared to be tables which were being laid for two persons.

Then before she had time to see anything more the man opened a door and said:

"Here her is, Ma'am, an' if her ain't as good as her says she is, her's a good liar!"

A little nervously Vanola entered what seemed to be a very luxurious Sitting-Room decorated with velvet hangings and furnished with three huge satin sofas which astonishingly were in three different colours— one sky blue, one coal black, and one a rich red.

At the far end of the room there stood an enormously fat, hideous woman.

Because Vanola was so ignorant of the world, she did not realise she was looking at the acknowledged Queen of London Night-Life, Kate Hamilton.

Everybody in London knew Kate, who was one of the sights for visitors from overseas, and who had entertained at one time or another every eligible man in the Social World.

She had not yet dressed in the finery she assumed later in the evening, and the emerald green silk gown she wore over a large crinoline had a torn hem and could have done with a wash.

Her face was painted and powdered, and she looked Vanola shrewdly up and down taking in every detail from the two huge eyes which dominated her thin face to her hair which seemed to gleam under her cheap bonnet in the light of the gas-lamps.

"Well, what do you want?" she asked in an aggressively preemptory tone.

"I heard . . . that you needed a . . . pianist," Vanola said in her soft, musical voice.

"I want a pianist, but I want a man," Kate replied.

"I can play better than most men."

"Is that your opinion?"

"No, it is my father's and . . ."

Vanola hesitated a moment, then decided that as she hated him he might as well be useful.

". . . and the Duke of Arkholme's!"

Kate's eyes, surrounded as they were with rolls of flesh, seemed to widen.

"The Duke of Arkholme? How do you know him?"

"I have played to him."

"Did he send you to me?"

"Certainly not! And I would not wish him to know that I am here."

As she spoke Vanola was certain that the Duke would never come to a place like this.

She suspected from what she had seen already that it was one of the Dance Halls that she had heard her father speak of scathingly, saying that the dancing that took place in them was deplorable, and they were only a meeting-place for those in search of immorality.

She did not know why she was so sure that this was where she was.

It was not exactly anything she had seen but what she felt in the atmosphere, and something in the way Kate looked.

"What is your name?" Kate asked.

"Vanola."

"Is that all?"

"It is the name I wish to use," Vanola replied.

She had made up her mind even as Kate asked the question that if her father's name was in the newspapers as the winner of Lord Arkholme's competition, she would not want to be connected with it simply because it might lead in some way to her coming in contact with him.

She had merely used his name to Kate because her instinct had told her it was her one chance of not being dismissed without being heard.

There was silence, and she thought she had failed. Then Kate said grudgingly:

"Well, I admit you might be useful seeing as I've no one to play for me tonight. But if you are no good, I'll chuck you out! Is that clear?"

"Perfectly clear," Vanola said.

"And if I get a man tomorrow you can go anyway! Women pianists are a trouble. They always want to be on the floor rather than sitting at the piano, which is their rightful place."

"All I want to do is play," Vanola said.

"Do you know the new tunes?"

"Some of them, and I also know the melodies of a great many foreign composers, which are a great deal gayer and more spirited than what is usually played in this country."

Again she was quoting from what her father had said, and Kate seemed to be impressed.

"Very well," she said. "I'll hear you, but if you have wasted my time I shan't be pleased."

Vanola looked round as if for a piano, but Kate merely sailed towards the door like a galleon before the wind and she followed.

They went towards the Saloon, Kate stopping on the way to speak in a furious voice to a man who Vanola saw was a waiter who had come from one of the small rooms.

"If you leave dirty glasses about," Kate said, "and the bed unmade as you did last night, you can leave without your wages!"

"Everything's tidy now, Ma'am," he said nervously.

"It had better be!" Kate replied ominously.

She walked on and the waiter scurried back into the room as if afraid.

Vanola drew in her breath. Then she lifted her chin proudly and thought she would not kowtow to anyone, not even this overwhelmingly gigantic woman.

Kate led the way to the Saloon, and now Vanola noticed what she had not seen before, that beside the platform on which there was the velvet chair stood an upright piano.

One glance at it told her that it was quite a good make. At the same time, when she sat down at it and played a chord she realised it needed tuning.

Kate moved onto the stage and sat down on the velvet chair and was waiting.

Because she felt it would give her courage and also be a tribute to her father, Vanola played the Hungarian folk-song which had awoken the Duke from his sleep.

The melody seemed to ring out and fill the empty room, and for a moment she forgot where she was and played thinking only of her father and of how handsome he had been before they came to London and had encountered despair and starvation.

Then as the tune finished she played one of Offenbach's most famous compositions and followed it by one of Strauss's popular waltzes.

Only as her hands dropped into her lap did she realise that everything depended now on whether she was approved of by the ugly and gigantic creature sitting on her velvet throne.

There was silence for a moment. Then Kate said:

"I'll give you a chance, but you'll behave yourself. It's not your job to fraternise with the customers, you understand that?"

"I understand," Vanola replied, "and as I told you, all I wish to do is to play."

She rose from the piano-stool and walked to stand below the dais looking up at Kate Hamilton.

The two women's eyes met and Vanola had the strange feeling that Kate now realised she was indeed what she needed as a pianist but was reluctant to take her on because she was what Evie, who had sent her there, called a 'Lidy.'

Then Kate said sharply:

"As I said, I'll give you a chance, but if someone better comes along you'll go, and make no fuss about it."

"Of course," Vanola agreed.

"I'll give you £5 a week, and you'll play from eight o'clock until we close, is that understood?"

"Thank you," Vanola said.

That sum was more than she was expecting, and she thought that this meant she could be independent as soon as she had paid back the Duke what she owed him.

"You've got something to wear?"

Kate's voice was sharp and Vanola knew by the expression on her face that not surprisingly she did not approve of the brown gown she was wearing at the moment.

"I will find something."

"You had better, but nothing too gaudy, mind you. You are not here to attract attention, except for the men's ears. Their eyes are not for you."

"I understand that . . . Ma'am."

There was a little pause before she added the last word, and as if Kate was aware of it, she said:

"It isn't easy to be hoity-toity when you are on your uppers, and politeness doesn't cost anything."

"No, Ma'am."

"Remember I told you that."

"I will remember."

"You can go now," Kate said rising from the velvet chair, "but be back here at eight o'clock sharp. You'll get something to eat during the evening, but no drinks. Is that clear?"

"Yes, Ma'am, and thank you."

As if she knew it was expected of her, and also with a touch of irony, Vanola dropped a small curtsey.

Then she turned and as she walked towards the door through which she had entered she had the feeling that Kate was watching her, but she did not look back.

Only when she reached the outer door which led into the street did the man in shirt-sleeves reappear to let her out.

"Ye've got it?" he asked.

"Yes!"

"Good! But it ain't easy here, I can tell yer that. With that hair yer're going to find it hard to keep the customers away, and if ye're too familiar her'll have yer out as sure as eggs is eggs!"

"She told me that."

"Well then, don't yer forget it, and if yer have any trouble with them yer just tell me. I'll deal with 'em, whether they be Princes or pickpockets!"

Vanola realised he meant to be kind.

"Thank you very much."

Then as he opened the door she hurried away in search of a shop where she could purchase a cheap evening-gown.

*   *   *

At eight o'clock precisely she was back at Kate Hamilton's and the Saloon looked very different from what it had a few hours earlier.

Now the whole room sparkled in the gas-lit lustres,

and the mirrors multiplied and re-multiplied the girls who were preening themselves in front of them.

Vanola was to learn later that Kate was famous for providing the most attractive girls of any Saloon in London out of hundreds who competed for the pleasure-seeking men of every class.

Kate herself had originally climbed the ladder of Strumpetry by standing partially naked in the *poses plastiques* which had been one of the most popular attractions twenty years earlier.

Because she had a quick brain and a good memory she soon learnt what attracted the wealthy young aristocrats as well as the greenhorns who came up from the country with plenty of money but very little sense.

She had gradually made her Saloon the most exclusive the most expensive and certainly the most attractive in the whole of the West End, and to Vanola it was more fantastic than anything she had anticipated.

The 'girls' looked so lovely in their pretty gowns with their hair elegantly arranged and the two commissionaries, one of whom was her friend who had let her in and who was known as 'Tom' to all and sundry, were so impressive in their flamboyant livery that it took her sometime to notice how common the pretty girls voices were and how unsteady many of the customers were on their feet.

At first she could not understand the object of the 'Supper Rooms' which were divided down the middle making an attractive place for two people to dine, but when the curtains were pulled back they revealed a silk-draped, fringed and lace bed.

On the first night all this was a mystery to her, and

she was only concerned with keeping the dancers swirling round to the sprightly melodies that she played for them.

Forgetting where she was, she was carried away by her father's compositions into a world where there was only the flower-filled steppes and the snow-peaked mountains.

It was not until nearly five o'clock in the morning that she suddenly felt so tired that she was afraid she might collapse, and realised how long she had been playing with only two short breaks.

Not only was her whole body stiff from exhaustion, but her fingers as well.

Then as she rose a little unsteadily to her feet wondering if she would ever find her way home, Kate said to her:

"You certainly got them dancing. Be here sharp at eight o'clock tomorrow night, and I'll keep you for a short while at any rate."

"Thank you . . . Ma'am," Vanola managed to say.

Then as she felt as if she must crawl on hands and knees towards the door as otherwise she would never reach it, Tom was beside her.

"Yer were a sensation!" he said. "Everyone were a-saying t'was the best music they've ever heard!"

Vanola was almost too tired to thank him, and he said:

"Here, I'll get yer a hackney carriage, and yer can got to bed and stay there until it's time to come back tomorrow night. Don't yer worry, the old woman's got a winner in yer, and her knows it!"

Because she felt so weak Vanola wanted to cry at his kindness.

Then as he helped her into a hackney carriage and told it where to go he said:

"Do as I tells yer, and yer worries are over!"

chapter five

LUCY, who was a very pretty girl, went up to the piano where Vanola was playing.

"'Is nibs wants the Polka!"

"Not again!" Vanola exclaimed.

"That's wot 'e wants," Lucy said, "and 'ere you are, for your trouble."

She put half a sovereign down on the end of the keyboard, and Vanola just glanced at it before she started playing.

The first night at Kate Hamilton's she had not understood that when a customer asked for a certain tune he was expected to pay for it.

In fact everything at Kate's was extra.

Vanola had therefore left without picking up several half-sovereigns which were placed either on top of the piano or at the end of the key-board.

The next evening Tom had said to her:

"'Ere—these are yers, and don't yer forget 'em 'nother time."

He placed four half-sovereigns into her hand and Vanola stared at them in astonishment.

"What are these for?"

"When yer plays a tune a Gent asks for, 'e pays for the privilege."

"But . . . I cannot take money like . . . that," Vanola exclaimed.

"It's yers, one o' the perks, so to speak," Tom explained, "an' if yer don't take it, one of 'em greedy waiters will. They're always on the look-out for a bit extra."

Vanola hesitated.

Everything in her blood rebelled against accepting tips as if she was a servant.

Then she told herself that if she did accept them she would be able to pay off her debt to the Duke more quickly than she had anticipated.

There was however quite a pause before she said to Tom:

"Thank . . . you. I can see I am very . . . ignorant about what . . . goes on . . . here."

"Yer'll learn!" he replied with a grin.

She certainly did learn a great deal in the next few days.

At first she was too shy and too tired to do anything but concentrate on her music. Then she began to re-alise what an extraordinary place she was in.

Everybody who arrived was scrutinised through eye-holes in the door by the two resplendent commissionaires, and were only admitted if they were known to the establishment or if they had been sponsored by somebody already accepted by Kate.

In the Saloon there were tables and chairs round the dance-floor where newcomers would sit, but on the dais on either side of Kate, looking enormous in her low-cut evening gown, were a large number of attractive young women waiting to amuse any gentlemen who arrived alone.

These Vanola learned were not only aristocrats straight from the smart Clubs of St. James's, but Officers of both Services, Professional men, University Students and young country Squires who were more quickly relieved of their money than anybody else.

She learned that Kate expected anyone who came to her Saloon to spend £5 or £6 or perhaps more, and her Supper Rooms were frequented by a better class of man and woman than any other in London.

Because they quickly saw she had no intention of competing with them, the girls on the staff, and there were a large number of them, were very pleasant to Vanola.

They told her stories of the strange things that had happened at the house, such as the occasion three years earlier when the King of Siam sent three Ambassadors to pay tribute to the Queen.

The British Government had installed them at Claridge's and shown them places of historic interest, but they had soon become bored and were finally conducted with suitable escorts to Kate Hamilton's.

The story of how the Chief Diplomat of Siam had ordered unlimited champagne for everybody and spent an enormous amount of money on other pleasures made it sound to Vanola very much like a fairy-story.

When she felt it safe to look around her she found a room full of tall, handsome men in evening-dress, many with side whiskers and huge moustaches, wearing their top-hats and either talking to the rouged, painted and flamboyantly dressed women or dancing with them.

She was well aware of how horrified her mother would have been at her being employed in such a manner.

At the same time, because Kate appreciated her playing and was determined she should not leave the piano, she kept a sharp eye on her, and Vanola felt safe.

If any man attempted to enter into conversation with her, Kate would shout at him from her velvet throne in a manner that was both embarrassing and intimidating

"Stop it, M'Lord!" she shouted at one nobleman who was trying to attract Vanola's attention. "You leave the pianist alone. She's here to play, and that doesn't mean games with Your Lordship. If you want a woman and a pretty one at that, you've a better choice here than in any other place in London."

By the end of the week Vanola found to her astonishment that besides her salary she had collected nearly £10 in tips.

This meant, she thought with delight, that she would be able to send to the Duke the money she had spent from his £50 on her father's funeral and her gown.

She had found a shop in Shaftesbury Avenue where the majority of the gowns seemed very gaudy, although one or two were more subdued and in good taste.

She thought first in order to be unobtrusive she would wear black, but with her white skin and red hair it made her look, even to her own eyes, so striking that she was sure it would be a mistake.

She had therefore chosen a gown with a small crinoline in a soft shade of blue which had a draped bodice and was not too *décolleteé*.

It was impossible to buy a gown without a crinoline and although Vanola at first was afraid it would make her more noticeable, she was aware that she might attract the people who frequented Kate's because she would look strange without one.

She brushed back her hair from her forehead as smoothly as possible, avoiding the curls and elaborate coiffures of the other girls, and twisting her red hair into a tight chignon at the back of her head.

She had no idea that because she looked so neat and at the same time so lovely the men found it hard not to look at her and look again.

Everybody who entered Kate's establishment realised that there were strict rules and to break them meant that they were very likely to be firmly escorted to the door by Tom and the other commissionaire who was as tall and strong as he was.

One thing Vanola had found gratifying in her desire to save money and spend as little as possible was that Kate provided excellent food for those she employed.

The Chefs who catered for the Supper Rooms also cooked what was eaten by the girls if they were not successful in getting a client to give them supper, as they were expected to do.

Supper for those who could pay for it, consisted of rich food washed down with very expensive wines and an unlimited amount of champagne.

Vanola did not like to think what was the purpose of the beds in the screened off part of the Supper Rooms, but there was no doubt they were extremely popular.

She learned that the girls vied with each other for the privilege of being allowed to go onto the dais beside Kate where they could be seen to advantage by any man arriving alone.

From the moment she became a pianist for Kate Hamilton, Vanola found that her whole life had changed.

Because she never got home until after five o'clock in the morning, she would sleep exhaustedly in the tiny bedroom at Mrs. Bates's, to wake at one o'clock or even later.

Because Mrs. Bates liked her she was allowed the privilege of cooking something to eat in her own kitchen in the basement.

As this was clean and very different from the cockroach-infested squalor of the kitchen in Praed Street, Vanola was sensible enough to realise that unless she was to play badly from sheer fatigue she must eat nourishing food.

She therefore bought herself steaks and lamb chops.

Although at first she found it hard after being hungry for so long to eat such heavy food, she managed to consume quite a decent amount and with the elasticity of youth begin within a few days, to feel very much better than she had for months.

If she arrived punctually at Kate's at eight o'clock she was then entitled to eat what the Chef had provided in a small room off the kitchen with the other girls who at this hour were usually in various stages of undress.

Vanola discovered that they usually arrived in their day-clothes, having left their evening-gowns in Kate's thereby ensuring that they were not crushed or damaged through being worn to and from their homes.

Sometimes a gentleman would leave with one of Kate's girls, but he had to pay heavily for the privilege, and it was not something she encouraged, asking in a truculent tone what he thought the Supper Rooms upstairs were there for.

Even though the girls before nine o'clock were not heavily made up with paint on their faces some of them were very pretty, and they were certainly pleasant to Vanola.

"If you wants to buy another gown," one of them said, "I'll tell yer where you can get really elegant ones, worn by the smartest Ladies in High Society."

"Do they sell their gowns when they have no further use for them?" Vanola asked in surprise.

"Not them, stupid!" the girl replied. "Their lady's-maids do, it's one of their perks, so to speak."

It was something Vanola had never envisaged and because she felt ashamed at arriving at Kate's looking so shabby and threadbare she went to the shop that had been recommended to her.

She found there what she knew had originally been very expensive and beautifully made gowns of every sort and description.

Some of them were still too much for her to afford, but she managed for a very small sum to buy a gown with a built-in crinoline that was not exaggerated, but exactly right for her.

It had a little jacket to go over it and a pretty bonnet that was very different from the dilapidated one which she had worn for so long that the ribbons were split and frayed so that it was difficult to tie them.

Even with this expenditure she would still have quite a lot to send to the Duke when she was paid at the end of the week.

She thought she would do as she had done before and give it to one of the small ragged boys who were always hanging about the streets to deliver to him.

She wondered what the Duke would think when he received it and was quite certain he would laugh at her for being proud.

When she thought of the luxury and the treasures she had seen in his house she knew that the money she was sending was as unimportant to him as a drop of water.

Yet because she was aware he was, in fact, in many ways very intuitive at least where she was concerned, she knew he would understand that she was paying him back because she held him responsible for the deaths of her mother and father.

"I hate him! I hate him!" she exclaimed and found herself pressing her fingers on the keys so violently that some of the customers in the Saloon turned their heads to look at her as if startled by the loudness of the music.

It was then, as she looked at them feeling apologetic because she had let her feelings supercede her musical sense, that she saw the Duke.

He was walking in through the door at the far end of the room accompanied by another man almost as elegant as himself.

He stood staring around him and Vanola quickly looked away wondering frantically how she could run and hide, and prevent him from seeing her.

* * *

The Duke and Brooky had spent yet another evening—and it was becoming monotonous—touring the night-spots of London where there was music.

Public Dance-Halls had become such a feature of night-life in the Metropolis and there were so many of them, that Brooky had said he was only surprised that any man after a week in London was left with a penny in his pocket.

After they had visited some places that were very low indeed and which he was quite certain no woman with any pretentions of decency would enter, he said:

"Oh, for God's sake, Lenox, let us go home! I am fed up with the dirt, the smell and the excruciating noise of these places. If you ask me, if Vanola is anything like your description of her, she would be frightened to put a foot inside any of them."

"I agree with you," the Duke said, "but where else can she be? And how else can she earn money?"

It was what he had asked himself and Brooky over and over again.

Mr. Carstairs had been instructed to get in touch with all the well-known Dance Academies and Dancing Teachers and find out if somebody answering Vanola's description had applied to them for employment.

In a discussion with Brooky the Duke had ruled out the idea of her approaching the Theatres.

"I do not know of a Theatre which employs women in the Orchestra," he said, "and I cannot imagine she would try to do a turn in a Music Hall."

He paused and as Brooky did not speak he went on:

"That leaves the Dance-Halls, and the only thing we can do is to go and look in them all and see if she is playing an Orchestra like they have at the Argyll Rooms, or the piano at Caldwell's in Dean Street.

"That is a fate worse than death!" Brooky remarked, but the Duke did not appear to be listening.

They had therefore set out to visit some of the hundreds of different places in London which catered to any man who was looking at the glittering, bright lights for amusement, and had the money to pay for it.

The Argyll Rooms was the most celebrated and had an excellent Orchestra, but the players were all men.

The entrance fee for the ground floor Dance-Hall was one shilling and it was crowded to suffocation. An extra charge was made for the Gallery where there were alcoves with plush-covered benches and, as Brooky quoted from some Methodist tract summed up, a large number of "bedizened or brazened-faced harlots."

At first Brooky found it all rather amusing.

For five shillings he bought a small paper-covered book called *A Swell's Night Guide to the Great Metropolis, Displaying the Saloons, the Paphian Beauties, the Chaffing Cribs, the Introducing Houses* edited by the Lord Chief Baron.

He laughed a lot as he read extracts from it to the

Duke, then realised somewhat to his surprise that his friend was not amused.

In fact, as their search continued Brooky realised to his amazement that the Duke was not only taking his search for Vanola very seriously, but was really worried and perturbed in case he did not find her.

Even allowing for his involvement with her father's music which was already displayed in the Music Shops, and causing, Brooky learnt, something of a sensation, he had never known the Duke to worry himself over any woman or to be actively concerned about her to the point where he seemed unable to take an interest in anything else.

Because it was so unusual Brooky tried to enter into the spirit of the search and be intelligent about it.

He suggested they went to places like the Coal Hole and the Cider Cellar. They even looked where there was open-air dancing, like Vauxhall and Cremorne.

When these proved to have large Orchestras who were all men they returned to the Dance-Halls, some of which were so rough that the Duke walked in and straight out again.

"We cannot go on doing this for ever!" Brooky protested when after dinner at Arkholme House which he found excellent while the Duke ate very little, they rose from the table and he learnt that a closed carriage was waiting for their visit, outside.

"If you do not wish to come with me," the Duke replied, "I will go alone."

"Of course I will come with you," Brooky answered. "At the same time I can think of more amusing

113

places than those we visited last night."

"I remembered this morning," the Duke said, "that we have not yet been to Mott's. It is supposed to be more select than the Argyll or the Holborn."

"Not in some people's opinions," Brooky replied. "It was at Mott's that Hastings turned off the lights and let two hundred famished sewer rats out onto the dance-floor!"

The Duke laughed, remembering the sensation the young Marquis's action had caused.

"It was something he would not do twice," he remembered, "so we will start at Mott's. But I have an idea they have quite a large Orchestra."

They had, but the Duke went on to look in at a large number of Dance-Halls in the Haymarket and Holborn and finally when Brooky was on the verge of revolt he exclaimed:

"I know where we have not been, and that is to Kate Hamilton's."

"You need not waste your time," Brooky replied. "Kate has quite a good pianist, who is a man, and I thought when I was there about three weeks ago that he played rather well."

The Duke however was determined and gave his orders and as the carriage drew up outside the entrance in Prince's Street Brooky groaned, but followed his friend up to the closed door through which they were inspected through the eye-hole.

Tom took only one glance at the tall, distinguished figure outside before he flung open the door.

"Evening, Yer Grace. It's nice to see Yer Grace back here again. 'Tis a long time since yer paid us a visit."

Before the Duke could reply Tom bowed to Brooky.

"Evening, M'Lord. Always a pleasure to see yer!"

Tom hurried along the passage and up the stairs in front of them to open the door into the Saloon.

There was the usual noise of voices and laughter. Then there came a sudden crash of chords on the piano which being somehow unexpected made several people look up as if in surprise.

The Duke's eyes followed theirs and as he did so he realised that his search was ended.

He was however too intelligent to walk straight to the piano to speak to Vanola.

There were a number of men in the room who either smiled at him or waved, and he was quite certain that Kate had noticed his arrival and would be delighted to see him.

He was also sure that Vanola would feel very differently.

That she had not been in touch with him after her father's award was announced told him all too clearly that she wished to avoid him, and one thing he did not want to do was cause a scene or trouble of any sort for her.

He therefore walked to the Bar which meant that for the time being he had his back turned to the rest of the room, and he hoped that Vanola would think he had not seen her.

The Bar was up-to-date enough to have mixed drinks which had been introduced in America and which Kate had caused quite a sensation by copying

There were strange mixtures going by such names as 'Gum Ticklers,' 'Eye Openers' and 'Cork Reviv-

115

ers,' but the Duke merely ordered a bottle of the best champagne and when he and Brooky had poured out a glass for themselves gave instructions for a bottle to be taken to Kate on the dais with his compliments.

This was such a usual procedure that the waiter hurried to obey, and when the Duke turned round Kate raised her large, fat arm and holding the glass high above her head, drank a toast to him.

He raised his glass to her in return, then walked from the Saloon with Brooky following him. As Vanola watched them go she gave a deep sigh of relief.

'He did not see me,' she thought, and felt her anonymity was still intact.

Without consciously intending to do so her fingers began to play the Hungarian folk-song which her father had composed and which she had played when she had awoken the Duke after climbing into his house.

After the Polka and all the other dance-tunes it seemed to have the sparkle of champagne, or the sharpness of the light on the snow and the sunshine from a cloudless sky.

For a moment there was chatting, talking and drinking in the Saloon.

Then almost despite themselves the people stopped to listen until as Vanola finished playing there was almost silence before nearly everybody began to clap.

She was so pleased at having eluded the Duke that her fingers had seemed to fly over the keys, and she was almost surprised when she found an hour or so later that the Saloon was nearly empty and the last customers, all very unsteady on their feet, were being helped down the steps by Tom and the other commissionaire.

She rose to her feet and shut the lid of the piano after first picking up the half-sovereigns that had been given to her during the evening.

There were rather more than usual, and she thought with delight that she would nearly have £10 to leave at the Duke's house in Park Lane tomorrow.

"Next week perhaps I can save more," she told herself.

Then as she collected her cape and put it over her shoulders she realised she was very tired.

Kate in her enormous crinoline glittering with jewels passed her in the doorway.

"Goodnight, Vanola," she said. "You played well tonight. But you'd better get yourself a new evening-gown. I'm getting tired of seeing that one."

"Another...one...Ma'am?" Vanola questioned.

She had the feeling Kate was only trying to find fault in case she got too 'uppity,' because she had been praised. And she had no wish to spend any more of her money on clothes.

"I expect everyone in my employment to look smart," Kate said, "not gaudy, that's a different thing where you're concerned, but I don't wear the same dress every night, and I don't expect you to."

Vanola wanted to argue that their roles were very different. Then she told herself it was stupid to upset Kate and risk losing her position as the pianist.

"I will do my best to find one tomorrow, Ma'am," she said meekly, and walked away down the now-empty Saloon where the waiters were extinguishing the gaslights.

Tom was waiting for her by the front door.

"I've got a carriage for yer outside," he said.

"Thank you, Tom," Vanola said gratefully, "I am

too tired to walk a single step."

"Yer don't have to do that."

Tom opened the door and Vanola, feeling as if she was already half-asleep let him escort her across the pavement and into the carriage that was waiting outside.

Only as she sat down on the back seat did she give a little scream as she realised she was not alone, and there was somebody else sitting beside her.

"It is all right," the Duke said quietly, "it is only I, Vanola."

"You!" Vanola exclaimed. "Why are you here? I thought Tom had got me a hackney carriage."

"I told him that I would take you home," the Duke said, "and may I say, Vanola, I have had a very hard time finding you."

"Why . . . why . . . should you . . . want to . . . find me?"

Because she was so astonished to find the Duke sitting in the carriage beside her she found it hard to be conscious of anything except that he seemed very large and overpowering.

At the same time in some way she could not explain to herself, she knew it was inevitable that he should have been aware that she was in the Saloon as she had been aware of him.

"How could you do anything so absurd as to disappear," he asked, "when you knew your father's music is at last being acclaimed for its brilliance?"

"My father is . . . dead."

"That is what I thought must have happened," the Duke answered. "I am sorry. I know how much it must have upset you."

She did not speak and after a moment he said:

"But I think he would be glad that his genius is

now apparent to everybody who hears those three wonderful compositions you left me."

"It is . . . too late!"

"Too late for what?" the Duke asked almost sharply. "Music is ageless, as you are well aware, and I cannot believe that your father would want what he had given to humanity to die with him."

Vanola stared ahead of her.

In the pale dawn light which was beginning to creep up the sky the Duke could see her profile against the window.

He was sitting almost sideways on the back seat to look at her and he knew she was thinking about what he had said. After a moment she replied hesitatingly:

"Perhaps I was . . . wrong . . . and Papa would want his music to . . . make people happy and . . . inspire them."

"Of course he would!" the Duke agreed. "I cannot believe that you, as a Hungarian, believe that death is the end, either for your father or for the music he has given to the world."

What the Duke said was so surprising not only to Vanola but also to himself that he ceased speaking, and she turned her head to look at him, her eyes very large in her small face.

"Do you . . . really believe," she said in a voice he could hardly hear, "that Papa is . . . still alive?"

"His spirit and his genius is something which will never die!" the Duke replied. "You are a musician, Vanola, and you know that what I am saying is the truth."

She clasped her hands together and after a moment she said hesitatingly:

"I suppose . . . because I have been so busy . . .

hating you...I did not think of Papa as being ...alive."

"I knew you hated me," the Duke answered, "and that is why, Vanola, I have taken the greatest pains to see that what occurred in the past will never occur again while I have any power as regards Music."

She did not speak and he thought there was a light in her eyes that he could see, or else he was intuitively aware of it.

"In a fortnight's time," he went on, "I am holding another audition for new compositions, and I hope that many who were turned away in the first place will attend it because it will take place in my Music Room in Park Lane."

Vanola held her breath.

She understood that in this way he was ensuring that there was no chance of any of those who brought him their compositions having to pay for the privilege of having them heard.

"That is very good of you," she said.

"I hoped you would think so," he replied. "I want you to have luncheon with me tomorrow and advise me on how we can arrange the room to hold everybody who applies, and whether you think it would be best for them to hear each other's compositions, or to wait in another room and come in front of the Judges one by one."

He did not wait for her to speak, but made a gesture with his hand as he said:

"There are those questions and a great many others on which I need your help and advice. I cannot risk another failure."

"Do you...really want...me?" Vanola asked.

"Of course I want you," he answered, "just as if

your father was with us I would ask him. But as, alas, he is not, I cannot ask his help. So I must have yours."

Vanola could hardly believe what he was saying, and yet she knew it made sense.

He was making reparation for the deplorable circumstances she had revealed to him, and she knew it would be impossible for her to refuse what he asked.

Yet she felt as if once again her whole world had turned a somersault and it was difficult to make coherent sense out of it, simply because it was so unexpected.

She knew he was waiting, and after a little while in a voice he could hardly hear and which seemed to her to come from a very long way away, she said:

"I . . . I will . . . try to help you . . . if you are quite certain that is . . . what you want . . . and if I am . . . really necessary."

"You are necessary as a musician," the Duke replied, "and especially as your father's daughter."

She felt it was so wonderful to hear her father spoken of in such a way, when she had never dreamt it was something that would happen.

Then the Duke said with an almost harsh note in his voice:

"How could you lower yourself to play in a place like Kate Hamilton's?"

Almost as if he brought her back to earth from the clouds on which she had been floating, immersed in her father's music, Vanola replied:

"I had to work . . . and I was very lucky that the pianist had been sacked for being . . . drunk."

"And you think that is the right sort of place in which to play your father's music?" the Duke asked. "Why could you not have let me arrange something

121

for you, as I wanted to do?"

She looked away from him and he said:

"All right, you hated me, that I can understand. At the same time, to prostitute your music and your ability to play in a way that few women can equal is a crime against everything in which you and I believe."

Vanola was so startled that she gave a little cry.

"How can you . . . say that to . . . me?" she asked. "It was a choice between either accepting your . . . charity, or . . . starvation!"

"That is not true," the Duke objected. "The money I gave you was your father's, and as you are well aware there is more than £1,000 of it waiting in his name to be collected. Perhaps you would like to tell me, Vanola, what you think I ought to do with it, for it belongs to nobody except you."

She did not answer and he went on:

"Also there is going to be a large accumulation of money in your name from the sale of the music which is now available in the Music Shops. And the Printers tell me they are already getting repeat orders and finding it hard to keep up with them."

"Is that true . . . really true?" Vanola asked in a strange voice.

"You know it is true, and you know it is something you have to deal with," the Duke said firmly. "So stop thinking of yourself, Vanola, but of your father."

There was silence and he knew that Vanola was fighting the tears that had come into her eyes.

He did not move, he only watched her until as the horses came to a standstill outside Mrs. Bates's lodging-house he said very quietly:

"I will send a carriage for you tomorrow at 12:30

P.M. Sleep until then, and think of nothing except that your father is not dead, but living in the hearts of all those who hear his music, just as he will always be in your heart."

He did not wait for Vanola to reply, but stepped out of the carriage to help her down onto the pavement.

The sky was now golden with the first rays of the sun, and it seemed to be reflected in Vanola's eyes.

She put out her hand, and the Duke took it in both of his.

Then as they looked at each other there seemed to be no need for words.

She was vividly conscious that his hands seemed to vibrate against hers and give her strength and a strange feeling of comfort she had never thought to find with him.

Then as she took her hand from his the door of the house opened and Billy, who was always on duty until the last lodger was in, stood there, wiping the sleep from his eyes.

"Goodnight," Vanola said in a voice that was little above a whisper.

"Goodnight," the Duke replied. "We will talk about everything tomorrow. Just think of your father, and trust me."

He turned away to walk back to the carriage, and as Vanola went up the stairs she felt as if she were in a dream.

chapter six

LUNCHEON was finished, and it seemed to Vanola as if everything about it had been part of a dream in which she had been enveloped ever since she had left the Duke last night.

She had fallen asleep with his words ringing in her ears, and it seemed to mingle with her father's music so that they were indivisible.

When she had woken up having asked Mrs. Bates to call her at noon she had the joyous, excited feeling that something wonderful was going to happen which she had not known, she thought, since she was a child.

She had her new pretty gown to wear which she had bought at the second-hand shop and a bonnet that was fashionable, and she knew on this occasion she would not feel so out of place in the Duke's magnificent house.

Before she was ready Billy came upstairs to say with his eyes popping with surprise:

"There's a reel smart carriage for ye, Miss Vanola, wi' two 'orses, an' two men to drive 'em!"

Vanola smiled, knowing that he was thinking of the footman on the box.

"Thank you, Billy!"

When she saw the horses she could understand Billy's surprise, just as she felt surprised by the long line of footmen in the Hall at Arkholme House and the high-ceilinged magnificent room into which she was shown.

The whole house, she thought as she sat at luncheon, was the right background for the Duke, and as they ate and talked she was vividly conscious of him, but in a different manner from the way it had been before.

Because he wanted to see her hair, although he did not say so, he suggested that she took off her bonnet as well as the little coat that went over her gown.

"It is warm today," he said, "and you will certainly be more comfortable."

She obeyed him without giving it a second thought, and now as she left the Dining Room ahead of him the sunshine through the window turned her hair to flaming gold, and he knew he had never seen a woman look more lovely.

They walked down the long passage which led to the Music Room on the other side of the house.

As they went into it Vanola gave a little exclamation.

It was exactly what she thought a Music Room should look like, with a small stage with marble pillars at each end and exquisitely executed murals behind the most superb piano she had ever seen.

Fashioned of rosewood it was ornamented and gilded and she knew without being told that the sounds which would come from it would be very different from those she had made on the piano at Kate Hamilton's.

The rest of the room was long and rather narrow with on one side windows opening onto the garden and the wall opposite also decorated with murals, and from the ceiling hung great crystal chandeliers.

At the far end a mirror framed in gold reflected the beauty of the whole room.

Without waiting for the Duke's permission Vanola walked to the piano and, as if she could not help herself, she bent over the key-board to strike a chord.

Then as the music of it seemed to vibrate within her she sat down on the piano-stool and began to play.

Without consciously thinking of it, almost as if her heart decided what the melody should be, she played one of her father's love-songs.

It was one the Duke had not heard before, and as he followed her to the dais he did not sit down but leaned against one of the pillars watching her face.

The music was, like all Sandor Szeleti's compositions, compelling, mesmeric from the first notes to the last.

He made the listener hear what he had to say not only with his ears, but with his instinct, his mind, and eventually his soul.

It was impossible not to become identified with the music which was so personal that the listener became a part of it, then was caught up with the glory and wonder of it, until the whole body vibrated.

Only as the notes, haunting and unforgettable, died away on the last chord did Vanola look at the Duke.

Her eyes met his, and she said in a voice that seemed to come from another world:

"Papa said that . . . was the 'Spirit of . . . Love.'"

Without waiting for the Duke to speak she went straight into another composition which, like the first one he had heard, conjured up a picture of wild grasses blowing in the wind, a river running silver through the centre of a valley, the snow-covered mountains peaking high into the sky.

It was so compelling that the Duke found himself not only seeing, but feeling as if the music opened for him new horizons and gave him new ideas which had never entered his head before.

Then as Vanola finished with a crescendo of notes that seemed to carry him into the sky did she say as she played the last chord:

"Papa said once that music should really be played in the open air and never . . . constrained or . . . encircled by walls. Then it is . . . exciting . . . romantic and . . . adventurous!"

She finished the last words with a smile on her lips, and was aware that the Duke was moving towards her.

Before she could move, before she could even think, he had lifted her from the stool, pulled her close against him, and his mouth came down on hers.

For a moment she was too astonished to realise what was happening.

Then as she thought she should struggle against him the pressure of his lips gave her feelings she had

128

never known before, and which was part of the music she had just played, only more insistent and more poignant.

She felt as if the sunshine burning over the snow-capped mountains was moving in her body, up through her breasts into her throat, then on her lips to become part of his.

It was so thrilling that she was unable to move or breathe, until as the Duke's lips became more possessive, more demanding, she felt as if the sunshine turned to lightning.

Flashing streaks that were so intense that they were half pain and half pleasure shot through her, making her quiver and at the same time feel a rapture she had never known existed.

The Duke kissed her until the Music Room swung dizzily around her and disappeared, and they were moving high into the sky above the mountains into the very heart of the sun itself.

It was so wonderful, so glorious, everything she had yearned for and heard in her father's music, that the perfection of it was somehow familiar, and yet more intense than she could ever explain.

She only knew this was love in all its majesty, love as she had dreamed of it, longed for and thought she would never find.

Yet now it was hers it was infinitely greater than the height, depth and breadth of her imagination.

Only when the Duke raised his head and she could feel his heart beating wildly against her breast did Vanola say incoherently:

"I . . . love you! How could I possible . . . love you when I thought what I felt was . . . hatred?"

"I loved you from the first moment I saw you," the /

Duke said. "Like you I did not realise it was love. I only knew you bewildered and intrigued me as no one has ever done before."

Then he was kissing her again, kissing her fiercely, possessively, as if he was afraid he might lose her and was making her acknowledge that she was his.

* * *

A LONG time later, or so it seemed, when they were both breathless, the Duke drew Vanola gently from the dais down onto the floor and towards a sofa against the murals.

They sat down, he with his arms still around her, and she put her head against his shoulder being unable to think, conscious only that her whole body was vibrating to the wonder of his kisses and the joy of knowing she was in his arms.

He kissed her hair.

"You are so beautiful, my darling!" he said. "I cannot tell you what tortures I have been through since you ran away from me, wondering if you were in danger from other men and I was not there to save you."

"I have been . . . safe because I was . . . playing," Vanola said in a small voice.

"In a place which you should not even know exists," the Duke said, and his voice was harsh.

He pulled her closer to him. Then he said:

"How can I bear to think of you associating with such people? Now it is all over, I will look after and keep you safe, and never again shall you be poor, unhappy and alone."

The way he spoke in a voice deep with passion

made Vanola look up at him with a little smile.

He was everything, she thought, she had always believed a man should be: strong, masterful, and yet to her kind, gentle and considerate.

"How...could I have ever...hated you?" she asked wonderingly.

"It is something I forbid you ever to do again," he said. "My darling, I will make you so happy that the love you think you have for me now will be a very pale reflection of the love I will arouse in you when we are together, and closer than we can be at this moment."

As the colour stole into Vanola's cheeks he said:

"I do not intend to wait or argue about anything. You are mine and from this moment you must leave everything in my hands."

As if what he said excited him he kissed her again, and only when his kisses became too insistent and too passionate did she put up her hands in protest. Instantly he raised his head to say:

"Forgive me, my darling, I will not be rough and frighten you, but you make me feel wild, or perhaps Hungarian is the word! At any rate I know that when I touch you it is very hard to remember that I am English."

She gave a little laugh. Then she said:

"This is what Papa would want you to feel, and what he expressed in his music."

"It is what I *do* feel," the Duke said, "and what, my precious one, I will make you feel tonight."

"T-tonight?" Vanola questioned.

"I told you I do not intend to lose you for one moment," the Duke said, "and so tonight I must take you to an Hotel until I can find among the many houses I own in London, one which can be made ready for you. My secretary will see to that. In the meantime, we will be together, and never, my precious, adorable little love, will you enter any place as reprehensible as Kate Hamilton's."

There was a puzzled look in Vanola's eyes.

"I . . . I do not understand."

"It is quite easy," he replied. "I will send a note to Kate on your behalf, saying that unfortunately you are prevented from playing there tonight, or any other night. To soften the blow I will enclose a sum of money which will doubtless assuage her anger at losing you."

"But you say that I . . . am to . . . go to an . . . Hotel?"

"That would be the best thing to do," the Duke said. "You understand, my darling, it would be a mistake for you to stay here, for that is something I should not do in my position."

He kissed her forehead before he went on:

"As I say, I own a lot of properties in London. The very nicest and most suitable house shall be yours and, if it is already furnished, we will redecorate it and furnish it as a frame for your beauty! It will be a place where we will be alone, and nothing and nobody shall ever disturb us! Then I will teach you to love me as I love you."

He put his fingers under her chin and turned her face up to his as he finished speaking, and she saw the fire in his eyes.

As he kissed her there were flames on his lips and her whole body melted into his she responded because once again the streaks of lightning were running through her.

But her mind had somehow disassociated itself

from the emotions he had evoked in her and was crying out in protest.

Only when the Duke was breathless and he let her go did he say:

"And now, my precious one, I am going to send you back to your lodgings to pack what clothes you have. Tomorrow I will take you to the best dressmakers in London and you shall have gowns that will frame your beauty and jewels which will glitter like the light in your eyes."

He stood looking at her for a moment. Then he drew her to her feet.

"I want you to stay here so that I can kiss you for the rest of the day," he said, "but I have a lot of arranging to do, and before we can dine together and talk about ourselves, I must let you go for the moment, although it is difficult to let you out of my sight."

They had reached the door of the Music Room and he stopped to kiss her again. Then without speaking they walked hand in hand down the corridor towards the Hall.

Only when they were at the end of it did the Duke say:

"I will send you back in my carriage, and it will call back for you and your luggage at seven o'clock. I will have everything arranged by then, but darling, the hours we shall be apart will seem like centuries."

He stopped still in the middle of the corridor to look down at her.

"It is impossible for me to tell you," he said, in his deep voice, "how much I love and want you."

Their eyes met, and it was difficult for either of them to look away. Then as if he forced himself to speak lightly, the Duke said as they walked on:

"One thing I must make quite certain of is that the best piano procurable is in your house so that you can play to me and, in your father's words, make me 'excited, romantic and adventurous.'"

There was no need for Vanola to reply because they had reached the Hall.

The Duke picked up the little jacket that went with her gown and helped her into it.

Her bonnet had been laid beside it on a chair. She put in on and regardless of what the servants might think he tied the ribbons under her chin.

When he had done so his eyes were on her lips and she felt as if he kissed her again, and the colour rose in her cheeks.

Then they walked together in silence through the open front door and down the steps to where the Duke's carriage was waiting.

He helped her into it, kissed her hand and said in a voice only she could hear:

"Until seven o'clock, my lovely one, and after that we will be—together."

Involuntarily Vanola's fingers tightened on his, and as if satisfied at her response he stepped back, a footman closed the carriage door, and the horses drove off.

For a moment Vanola could only think of the beating of her heart, the pulsating of every nerve in her body, and that her lips could feel the Duke's mouth possessing them.

Then slowly, as if a bitter wind came from the North driving snow-clouds before it, the sunshine left her body, her dream ended and she faced reality.

The reality was that what the Duke had offered her was not the love she sought, the love that her mother had known with her father, or the love her father wrote into his compositions.

Instead it was what she had seen and shrank from in Praed Street.

It was Evie and her painted face and the crimson feathers in her bonnet, and the expression in the men's eyes as they looked at Kate Hamilton's girls.

It was also the Supper Rooms with their curtains hiding a frilled bed.

Vanola gave a little cry which was that of an animal who was mortally wounded, and put her hands up to her eyes.

Only when she realised that the horses had come to a standstill outside Mrs. Bates's lodging-house did her pride make her hold up her head as she stepped from the carriage and thanked the footman in a quiet, calm voice.

Then as Billy opened the door to her she ran up the stairs frantically as if all the devils of hell followed her.

In her room she packed her small trunk, having very little to put in it except for the evening-gown she had worn at Kitty Hamilton's and a few small trinkets which had belonged to her mother.

Then when her trunk was strapped down she went downstairs to the kitchen to find Mrs. Bates.

"You're leaving us, Miss?" Mrs. Bates asked. "Well, that is a surprise! I thought you was 'appy 'ere."

"I have been, and you have been very kind," Vanola replied, "but I have to leave London...unexpectedly and I hope you will...forgive me for giving you such short...notice."

She knew by the expression on Mrs. Bates's face

what she was thinking, but somehow it did not matter. It was just part of the nightmare.

It had swept away her happiness so completely that she felt it had never been there, but had only been an illusion, a mirage with no substance in fact.

Billy got her a hackney carriage and put her trunk in the front of it.

"Thank you, Billy, for all you have done for me," Vanola said.

She gave him a sovereign and as she stared at it incredulously, she added:

"Do not let anybody take it from you."

The hackney carriage carried her away while he was still staring at the coin he held in his hand, as if he thought it could not really be there.

Only when the hackney carriage was a little way down the road did the cabman turn round to say:

"Yer ain't told me where yer're a-goin', but I s'pose, seein' as yer're taking' some luggage, yer're awaiting the Stage Coach."

Vanola drew in her breath, then as if she was taking the plunge into some icy water she replied:

"No, I want a Post Chaise. Please take me to a stable that has the best and fastest."

She thought as she spoke there was a hard note in her voice that had never been there before.

At the same time, her heart was crying for the mirage which had vanished, leaving her in a waterless desert which stretched away into eternity.

* * *

The Duke, having arranged everything to his satisfaction which had necessitated cancelling a long list of engagements including what had seemed when he accepted it, quite an important dinner for that night, waited impateintly for Vanola's arrival.

Mr. Carstairs had his instructions as to the Hotel at which they would stay since it catered for anyone who wished to remain anonymous with a discretion which had made it famous.

It was not the place he really wished to take Vanola, but at least they could be comfortable and together.

Mr. Carstairs had promised that by tomorrow the house in St. John's Wood which the Duke had owned for some years would be staffed with servants and ready to receive them.

Like many wealthy men in London, the Duke owned quite a number of houses which he let, thereby increasing his already large income, but there were just two or three which he kept for himself and in which, when it suited him, he installed a mistress.

It was of course the fashion for every nobleman to have what was known as a 'Cyprian,' or a 'Pretty Horse-Breaker' as his disposal.

But while on the whole the Duke preferred an *affaire de coeur* with a Society Lady, he occasionally took a singer or a dancer from Covent Garden under his protection, although they seldom amused him for any length of time.

He would not have thought of asking Vanola to stay in a house where he had kept another woman.

She was so different from anybody he had ever known before and so precious that he was already planning that the house they would share would be so exceptionally beautiful that it would be a fitting Temple for their love and nothing in it should jar their senses.

The house in St. John's Wood, according to Mr. Carstairs, was large and stood in its own garden. Although that part of London was associated with the mistresses of wealthy gentlemen, the Duke thought that in a more respectable neighbourhood the sight of his carriages embellished with his crest might cause comment.

He had no wish to add more fuel to the fire of the gossip-mongers.

"You are quite certain the house is really a good one?" the Duke had asked of Mr. Carstairs.

"I promise Your Grace it is one of the most attractive houses in the neighbourhood."

"I will see it myself in the morning," the Duke said, "but go ahead and make arrangements for it to be properly staffed and later I will tell you what pictures I would like moved there from here, and perhaps some of those at Holme Park."

Mr. Carstairs was too wise to comment, but he looked surprised, since in all his years of serving the Duke he had never known him to take anything from the houses in which he lived to one in which he wished to install a mistress.

At the same time, he could not help noticing that the Duke looked happier than he had seemed for a long time.

There was something vital and alert about him which made him seem much younger, and his face had lost that air of disdain which many people found intimidating.

'He is in love!' Mr. Carstairs thought with astonishment, though he could hardly believe it could be true.

At seven o'clock the Duke was waiting in the Salon. He had changed into evening-dress and had decided that he and Vanola would dine here in Park Lane before they left after dinner for the quiet Hotel.

It would have been just as easy to dine in their Sitting-Room there, but with a perception that was unusual he thought it might in some way remind Vanola of Kate Hamilton's Supper Rooms.

He had very occasionally in the past used them himself, and knowing they were very popular with his contemporaries he could not help wondering what Vanola had thought of them, and if she had been shocked.

There was a frown between his eyes as he realised that so much of what she had seen at Kate's must have been upsetting, perhaps horrifying, to a young girl who, as far as he knew, had always been chaperoned either by her father or her mother, and had never until Sandor Szeleti's death been on her own.

He had a feeling however, simply because there was an inescapable aura of purity about Vanola, that much of what had happened around her, even at the disreputable Boarding House in Praed Street, might have been incomprehensible.

"'To the pure, all things are pure,'" he quoted to himself, but at the same time felt uneasy.

Then he thought angrily that she should never have been involved in anything so sordid, so unsavoury, as Praed Street and Kate Hamilton's and with having to earn her living by playing in what Brooky had bluntly described as a 'Whore Market.'

She would not understand what it was all about, he told himself again, but still was doubtful.

"She is very young and she will forget," he said to reassure himself, and went on planning the gowns he would give her and the jewellery he would clasp around her neck and wrists.

Even to think of Vanola made his heart seem to vibrate in his breast and the blood throb in his temples.

He wanted her, not only because she was so beautiful and excited him, but also, he thought, because her music lifted his heart and mind in a way no one had ever done before.

He suddenly felt as if new ideas and ambitions were awakening within him.

He found himself thinking of speeches he would make in the House of Lords, reforms he would advocate and fight for, and new ways in which he could serve his country instead of spending all his time in seeking pleasure.

"When we are together," he said aloud, "we will also revolutionise the Music World!"

As his voice seemed to ring out the door opened and the Duke turned round eagerly to greet Vanola. But it was Newman who stood there and when he did not announce her the Duke asked:

"What is it, Newman?"

"The carriage has returned, Your Grace, but Miss Szeleti had left the house where she was staying."

"What do you mean—left?" the Duke asked sharply.

"The landlady, Your Grace, informed Johnson who was driving the carriage that the young lady departed half an hour after she returned there this afternoon."

"I do not believe it!" the Duke said angrily. "Miss Szeleti was aware that the carriage was calling for her at seven o'clock."

"Johnson waited until seven-thirty, Your Grace, but since the proprietress was quite certain that Miss

Szeleti would not be returning as she had taken her luggage with her, he had come back now to report."

The Duke was silent.

Then he knew, almost as if he was hearing a voice telling him so, that he had lost Vanola, and this time for ever!

*   *   *

Vanola was at that moment arriving in a Post Chaise at a large Georgian mansion on the outskirts of St. Albans.

It had taken her a little over two hours to travel there from London, and every inch of the way had made her more afraid of what awaited her, and more and more miserable with an utter despair at leaving the Duke behind.

At the same time she knew there was nothing else she could do, unless she was to become in her own eyes a traitor to her father's music and the ideals that her mother had instilled in her ever since she had been born.

"How can I become like Lucy, Molly, Daisy, Lily, or Gladys?" she asked, seeing the girls at Kate Hamilton's passing before her eyes one by one.

Because her music surrounded her with a wall of separation from them they had never quite seemed real.

While she talked to them and thanked them for their kindness, her mind had remained apart and known they were to her as 'Untouchables,' alien to everything in which she believed.

They were, she thought now, the natives of a foreign land to whom one behaved kindly, but with whom one had nothing in common.

Now the Duke was inviting her to become one of them, and she knew she would rather die than surrender the only thing she had left, which was her pride.

It was growing dusk with the last rays of the sun crimson against the sky, and she thought in contrast the house just ahead of her was dark and somehow menacing.

Then she knew it was only her own fears that made her feel like that, and she had heard her mother talk about it in a very different way.

The Post Chaise came to a halt below a long flight of grey stone steps and Vanola stared at them feeling it was almost impossible for her to move.

She knew that what she really wanted was the comfort of the Duke's arms and her whole being cried out for him. However badly he had behaved towards her, she knew he had aroused within her an unquenchable love that would never die.

"There is nothing I can do about it now," she said, and knew she was being tempted by the Devil and she must not listen.

A footman opened the door and with a dignity that she had learned as a child she managed to say to the driver of the Post Chaise:

"Will you please wait? I think I shall be staying here, but I am not quite certain."

"Oi gotta get back t'London, Lidy," he answered in a somewhat surly tone.

At the same time she knew he was impressed by the grandeur of the house and the number of servants who were appearing at the top of the steps.

She walked slowly up them, until outside the front

door an elderly Butler was waiting with white hair and an expression on his face which told her he was surprised to see her.

"I wish to speak with the Earl of Sandridge."

"I don't think, Ma'am, that His Lordship's expecting you."

"No, I have no appointment," Vanola replied, "but will you please tell His Lordship that his granddaughter Vanola is here to see him?"

She saw the Butler's eyes open in surprise. Then he said:

"You can't be, Miss! You're not Lady Melina's child?"

Vanola smiled.

"Yes I am."

"Her Ladyship's with you?"

"My Mother . . . died early this year."

"I'm sorry to hear that, very sorry," the Butler said. "It's never been the same since she left and we all loved her."

Vanola felt the tears come into her eyes.

"Thank you for saying that," she answered, "and now perhaps you will ask His Lordship if he will see me."

She knew without being told that the Butler was apprehensive as he walked across the Hall in front of her.

He turned towards a door on the right, then as if he changed his mind he said:

"I think, Miss Vanola, you'd best come with me and see His Lordship for yourself."

Vanola did not reply and followed him to another door, a double one of polished mahogany with gilt handles and doorplates.

The Butler walked slowly in front, almost as if he drew in his breath as he did so, and said in a stentorian voice that seemed to echo round the room:

"Miss Vanola to see you, My Lord!"

For a moment Vanola thought the large Library which she had entered was empty. Then she saw by the huge marble fireplace at the end of it there was a bowed figure sitting in a chair.

At first she found it impossible to move, for she had always thought of her grandfather, from all she had heard about him, as being large and overbearing, and later vindictive and cruel.

But the man in the chair seemed, because he was so old, very small and frail. His hair was white and the eyes that turned towards her were, she knew, finding it hard to focus as she approached him.

When she finally reached his chair to stand beside him he asked:

"Who are you? What did Danvers say your name was?"

"My name is Vanola, and I am your grand-daughter!"

There was a moment's silence. Then the Earl asked, and his voice was harsh:

"Did your mother send you to me?"

"My mother is . . . dead," Vanola replied. "She died last winter because it was so cold and we had not enough . . . money to buy the food and warmth she needed."

She spoke clearly because she wanted her grand-father to know the truth, but she was aware that he stiffened and now his eyes were searching hers as if he could hardly believe what he had heard.

"Dead!" he said almost beneath his breath as if he could not believe it was true.

"Yes . . . Mama is . . . dead," Vanola repeated, "and I have come to you, Grandpapa, because I . . . need your help."

"Why should you need that?" he asked, and now his tone was hostile. "Cannot your father look after you?"

"Papa also is dead," Vanola answered. "When he came to England the cold and the lack of food crippled him so that he could not play his violin! I think the truth is he died of . . . starvation."

She saw that her words had startled the Earl. Then he said almost as if he forced himself to speak harshly:

"And what am I expected to do about it now? Your mother left me for an Hungarian fiddler and, as I told her at the time, I no longer considered her my daughter."

"But I know you must have . . . missed her," Vanola said. "And I . . . miss her too."

She looked at the old man. Then suddenly, as if her instinct told her what to do, she went down on her knees beside him.

"Please be kind to me, Grandpapa," she begged, "and let me stay with you for a . . . little while. I have no money . . . and I am very afraid that on my own I might do something wrong . . . and of which Mama would not . . . approve. I have . . . nowhere to go . . . and I . . . belong to . . . no one."

She almost added: "at the moment."

Then she knew that her mother had brought her here, and her mother had prompted her to do what was right however hard it might be.

145

Now because her face was level with his and he could look at her, after a moment the Earl said as if he spoke to himself:

"Your face is like your mother's, and your eyes, but not your hair!"

"I am very happy to look like Mama," Vanola replied, "and I try to think like her. I know that she . . . wanted me to come to you because now that Papa is dead . . . I think this is the place I . . . should be."

"Your mother left here without any heart-burnings."

The bitterness in his voice and the raw tone in his words told Vanola how much her mother had hurt him.

"I know it must have upset you," she said quickly, "but Mama was very, very happy until when we came to England things went wrong. We had no . . . money . . . and no one wanted to . . . hear Papa's music."

She saw a frown between the Earl's eyes as she mentioned her father.

Suddenly she felt it was all hopeless and he was going to turn her away. She would have to go back to London, and either accept what the Duke had suggested or else return to play at Kate Hamilton's, or some place like it.

Even as she thought of it she knew that if the Duke took her in his arms and kissed her as he had kissed her this afternoon she would weakly do anything he wanted, and it would be impossible to resist him.

Her love, she thought, would make the sacrifice of her pride worthwhile.

Then she realised what she would become and what

her mother would feel if she was living, however luxurious it might be, a life of sin and degradation.

As if her whole body revolted at the idea she moved impulsively nearer to her grandfather and put her hand on his knee.

"Please ... please ... Grandfather ... help me!" she begged. "I am ... frightened of being ... alone ... and of the future ... I cannot manage by myself."

Her voice broke on the words and because she was so frightened that he would send her away the tears in her eyes overflowed and ran down her cheeks.

But still she looked at him, still pleading for him to understand.

He stared at her for a long moment. Then he reached out his hand and placed it on her shoulder.

"You are my granddaughter," he said slowly as if he was working it out for himself. "And this is where you should be!"

chapter seven

BROOKY walked into Arkholme House, and, as the
Butler took his hat and cane he said:

"His Grace is in the Music Room, M'Lord."

It was what Brooky expected, for ever since the
Duke had lost Vanola he had either been searching
for her in the highways and byways, and the Dance-
Halls of London, or else sitting alone in the Music
Room playing her father's compositions over and over
again.

Sometimes when Brooky heard the same melodies
played on the hurdy-gurdies in the streets or whistled
by every errand-boy, he thought it would drive him
mad.

But he knew it was not the music that was upsetting

him but his anxiety for the Duke and what he could do about it.

He had never in his whole long friendship with the Duke known him to behave in such a manner that was utterly uncharacteristic of him.

Gone was his calm, distant contempt for other people, and most of all his cynicism.

Now he was a man suffering in a way which seemed to Brooky incredible and yet at the same time he could understand it.

Of all the men he had ever known the Duke was the last one he would have expected to fall in love so deeply that his whole attitude to life was changed. He knew that until the Duke found Vanola again, he would not be a whole or complete man.

If the Duke had lain awake night after night, so had Brooky, wondering how he could help, wondering where on earth Vanola could be, and why she was behaving as she was.

For a week the Duke's natural reserve had made him keep to himself the reason for her leaving him. Then at last he broke down and told Brooky the truth.

"I swear to you," he said in a voice that did not sound like his own, "it never entered my mind that I should have asked her to be my wife."

He paused before he went on, as if he was thinking it out for himself:

"I suppose because I have always felt an abhorrence of being married, and because my relations have never stopped telling me how important it is that that I should produce an heir, I disliked the whole idea and shied away from it like a startled horse."

He did not tell Brooky how a revelation of what had happened had come to him the night after Vanola had disappeared, almost as if she was explaining it to him in her soft, musical voice.

Then he realised what a fool he had been and how, through sheer stupidity and perhaps too because he had always been so conscious of his high rank as an aristocrat, he had not understood.

When he did, he knew that what he had offered Vanola had offended and insulted not only her purity and the ideals that were expressed in the music she played him, but also his own ideals which he had once held, but which somehow had become forgotten in the superficial gaiety of the Social World in which he moved.

The love that he now knew he had for Vanola showed him how despicably he had behaved, and how he had forgotten her purity, innocence and childlike faith in his desire for her as a woman.

It was then that the Duke went down into a Hell of his own making, and suffered the agony of the damned until at times he thought he would go insane.

"Why did I not understand? Why did I not realise that she was utterly different from any woman I have ever known?"

He thought of the long stream of those who had passed through his life enticing him, doing everything in their power to incite his desire, flattering him and always acutely conscious that he was a Duke as well as a man.

He had known when he kissed Vanola that it would not have mattered what was his position in life.

They were two people who had found each other across time and space, who belonged to one another with their hearts and souls, and whose Social position was of no consequence.

151

"Fool! Fool! Fool that I was!" the Duke cried out in the darkness.

As night after night he was haunted by the spectre of his own stupidity he felt he was like a man who had held the most precious treasure in the world in his hands, but had lost it through sheer carelessness.

But in his mind a determination and an unquenchable pride which was the equal of Vanola's made him tell himself he would not be defeated.

He would find her again, implore her to forgive him, and ask her on his bended knees to honour him by becoming his wife.

It was to his credit that he never for a moment thought that Vanola was not good enough to become his Duchess. He only knew that he could not live without her and if he lost her for ever his own life would come to an end.

This was not only love in all its majesty, omnipotent, irresistible and unconquerable, it was also the agony of a crucifixion.

At first Brooky could hardly believe it was happening. Then because he loved and admired the Duke he strove by every means in his power to help him.

"Surely," he had said to Mr. Carstairs, "one of your investigators, ex-Policemen or whatever they are, must have some means of finding Miss Szeleti?"

"They's certainly trying to, M'Lord," Mr. Carstairs had replied in a worried voice. "I've a dozen of them now, but so far they have found no trace of the young lady anywhere in London."

"How can one woman disappear so completely?" Brooky had asked angrily.

Then he knew that among the seething hordes of

people in the Metropolis it was not really a very difficult thing to do.

Now he had news, and as he hurried down the passage to the Music Room he could hear the Duke playing her father's composition which Vanola had told him was a sound of love.

He was almost running as he pulled open the door, and he did so noisily so that the Duke who, when he was playing was almost indifferent to anything else that happened, turned his head in surprise.

Then as he saw the expression on his friend's face his fingers dropped from the key-board and he asked sharply:

"What is it? What have you heard?"

Brooky did not answer. He merely walked across the room and held out a piece of paper.

"I have found her!" he said. "But I do not know if you will be particularly pleased with what you will read."

For a moment it seemed as if the Duke was almost afraid to take what Brooky was holding out to him, and his friend went on:

"This is a letter from my aunt who lives near St. Albans in Hertfordshire. Read what it says, and you will understand why we could not find Vanola."

The Duke took the letter from him and for a moment the thin, spidery female hand-writing swam in front of his eyes.

Then he forced himself to read what was written on the crested writing-paper.

"My dearest Brooky,
   I am sending this to you by a groom because

I feel it is very important that you should be present at your Uncle's Wedding, which is to take place in two day's time, on Thursday.

I know it will be a surprise to you, and perhaps not a pleasant one, as I think you had expectations from my brother Edward. But after all these years of remaining a bachelor he is to be married. Although it has astonished us all that he should do such a thing, we must naturally support him.

It is a strange story, and I suppose in a way a romantic one. I expect you will remember that the Earl of Sandridge lives about three miles away from us in a large early Georgian house where you sometimes went to parties when you were a child.

The Earl had one daughter who was very beautiful, and although we were not aware of it at the time, your Uncle Edward fell in love with her when she was only a School-girl.

As he was thirty-seven or thirty-eight at the time, it was obviously impossible for him to be accepted by the Earl as her suitor, but because your Uncle insisted on courting her, the Earl took Melina with him to Hungary when he went to represent the Queen at the Wedding of Prince Esterhazy.

Apparently, while she was there, Melina fell wildly in love with an Hungarian musician.

I am told the Esterhazys were great patrons of music. At the same time, the musicians kept their place and the Prince was as horrified as the Earl when Melina ran away with an Hungarian with an unpronounceable name.

From that moment on the Earl would never speak to his daughter again, and as far as he was concerned she did not exist.

What your uncle felt about it I do not know for he did not confide in me. But he never married, and he never forgot her.

A month ago Melina's daughter suddenly appeared at Sandridge House and the Earl forgave the behaviour of her mother who is now dead, and has accepted her as his granddaughter.

To cut a long story short, your Uncle has proposed to the daughter of the woman he loved twenty years ago, and although it seems extraordinary, seeing the difference in age, the Earl has given his consent and they are to be married on Thursday.

Vanola, for that is the girl's name, is very lovely, but when I met her the other day she did not seem to be very happy, although perhaps it is just her foreign blood that makes her like that.

Everything has happened very quickly, and it seems to me extraordinary that your Uncle and this young girl should not have a long engagement to make quite sure they are not making a mistake.

At the same time the Earl is in very bad health, and I think he feels that if he dies, as I believe he might do at any moment, his graddaughter will be safe with your Uncle, and I think that is the reason for such a precipitate marriage.

Anyway, Dear Boy, I feel you will understand

155

*that we must rally round Edward and support
him even though, as you can imagine, a great
number of our relations think he is far too old
to embark on a new life with such a very young
bride.*

*Please therefore try to be at my house in time
for a light luncheon on Thursday at about noon.
The wedding is to take place that day in the
Village Church of Sandridge at two o'clock.*

*I look forward to seeing you, and I feel
sure you will want to come and support your
Uncle.*

I remain, your affectionate Aunt,
Denise Brook."

The Duke read the letter through slowly, then as
he came to the end of it Brooky said:

"I am sorry, Lenox."

"Sorry?" the Duke exclaimed and there was a note
in his voice that was almost like a trumpet-call.
"Thank God we have found her!"

"But, Lenox, you cannot upset the marriage at the
last moment. And for all you know she may love this
man."

Even as he spoke Brooky knew the Duke was not
listening.

There was a light in his eyes and it seemed suddenly
as if the lines had gone from his face. He looked
younger, alert, and had an air of urgency which
Brooky had seen before when he was going into battle.

Then as he rose from the piano-stool he said:

"I can never thank you enough, Brooky, for finding
Vanola for me! But now you have to help me."

*   *   *

As Vanola came slowly down the staircase at Sandridge Park she felt as if the veil over her face separated her from the world and she was moving as if in a dream that had nothing to do with reality.

She had in fact felt like that ever since coming to live with her grandfather.

At night she cried bitterly and despairingly into her pillow for the Duke: in the day she became a puppet which moved its arms and legs, which spoke when it was spoken to, but whose mind seemed somehow to have ceased to function.

Sometimes she felt as if she had left Vanola Szeleti in London, and the girl who appeared to live and breathe in Sandridge Park was no more than a cardboard dummy without any life in her body or her brain.

Somehow each day had begun and each day had ended without her feeling anything except an emptiness that made her think she had died and was now merely a ghost haunting the house where her mother had lived as a girl.

When she went into her mother's rooms which were just as they had been left, she felt as if her mother was near her and she cried out:

"Help me, Mama! Help me! Tell me if I have made . . . a mistake and I should have . . . stayed with the Duke and not . . . left him."

She thought of how her mother had given up everything for love, and when she compared the miserable room in which she had died with the grandeur and luxury of her grandfather's house she questioned for a moment if it had been worthwhile.

But then she had realised that the rapture, the wonder and the glory of her mother's love for her father and his for her was worth all the suffering, the cold and the hunger from which they had both died.

"Perhaps I should have found the same," Vanola argued to herself.

Then she knew her choice had been different.

She would not have given up luxury for real love, but for a love which was sordid and wicked, a degradation which would eventually prevent her from ever holding up her head again.

When Colonel Edward Brook had come to talk to her about her mother she had welcomed him, wanted to hear what her mother had been like when she was living in this huge house.

The Colonel had told her how beautiful she was and how everybody had admired her and she pressed him to tell her more, begging him to come again.

She wanted to hear about the old days simply because it made it easy to imagine her mother moving about the house, riding in the Park, and it fitted in with the stories she had been told about her mother's girlhood before she had gone to Hungary and met her father.

It was only a fortnight after she came to live with her grandfather that Colonel Edward Brook had asked the Earl if he could pay his addresses to his granddaughter.

The Earl had acquiesced because, Vanola thought, half the time he was thinking of her not as herself but as her mother, and he had also expressed his worry as to what would happen to her when he died.

158

"It will be difficult for me to provide you with anything but very little money, my child," he said one evening when he was speaking clearly and more sensibly than usual. "Everything I possess goes to my two sons, your uncles. One of them is in Khartoum as Governor of the Sudan, and the other is Viceroy of Ireland."

Vanola did not speak and the Earl sighed as he added:

"They both have large families and both complain that they never have enough money to make ends meet!"

"I would not wish them to think I had deprived them of anything that was theirs," Vanola said quickly.

Even as she spoke she wondered how she would manage if she had to go back to earning her living.

"One of our relatives will look after you, of course," the Earl said, "and I will manage to find you enough so that you at least will not be living on their charity."

It did not sound a very cheerful prospect, and as the Earl seemed to think it was a perfect solution for her to marry Colonel Edward Brook, who was a wealthy man with a large estate, Vanola weakly agreed.

She did not think of him as a husband so much as a father-figure, who would be kind to her and would take the place of her grandfather.

Because he was very humble in asking her to become his wife and made no demands upon her, kissing her hand or her cheek rather than her lips, she was not afraid of him.

159

She only felt that if she could not marry the Duke, then what happened in the future was not of any particular consequence.

Only when she played the piano could she escape into the magical world where the Duke's lips had taken her, but because it made her so unhappy she could not play the love-song which she had told him was the melody of music.

Instead she played the other two compositions, which had won the Duke's award, and several others which she busied herself in writing down from memory.

It took her some time because she was so afraid that she would miss some of her father's notes and the magic he infused into everything he composed.

But gradually as she played them over and over again, she thought they were exactly as he had written them, and she wanted with a longing that was a physical pain to play them to the Duke.

'Perhaps one day I will be able to send them to him, and he will have them published,' she thought.

But even to think of him was like thrusting a dagger into her heart, and just before her wedding she could not find any solace even in her music.

She therefore shut the lid of the piano and told herself that part of her life was finished for ever.

Now as she took a few more steps down the stairs she asked herself what she was doing, and where she was going.

Just for a moment her calm seemed to break and she thought with a sudden panic that she must run away.

"How can I marry a strange man? How can I go

away with him and bear his name when I belong to the Duke?"

Then she remembered that yesterday after the doctor had called to see her grandfather he had taken her on one side to say:

"His Lordship's growing very frail, Miss Vanola."

"His mind seems to wander a little more than it did when I first came here," Vanola replied. "All day yesterday he thought I was my mother."

"So many old people live in the past," the doctor said, "but at least it has made him happy having you here, and I think you're sensible enough to realise that His Lordship's happy for you to be settled with his old friend who'll look after you when he's gone."

This was what Vanola knew had been at the back of her grandfather's mind.

At the same time, only by thinking of her marriage as if it was happening to somebody else could she contemplate the idea of it and of making the vows which would tie her to Colonel Brook for ever.

'I cannot do it, I cannot!' she thought now.

Then she knew there was no alternative.

For one moment she thought that even now she would run away to London, tell the Duke she loved him and that nothing else mattered except their love.

Then she remembered almost as if she could see them in front of her the expressions in the eyes of the men at Kate Hamilton's as they looked at the girls on the dais, a way, Vanola thought, no man had ever looked at her, or if he had she had not been aware of it.

She was suddenly terribly afraid that she might see the expression in the Duke's eyes, and know that what he felt for her was not love, but something very different; something so horrible that she shrank from it because it was evil and unclean.

"That is what he offered me," she told herself, and tried to remember what she had felt when she had hated him because she believed it was his fault that her father and mother had died, and his fault that there was corruption and bribery at his Competitions.

But all she could remember was the note in his voice when he said he loved her and the way his lips had carried her up into the sky.

She had thought that he gave her the sun, the moon and the stars, and they were enveloped by the music of the spheres and the light that came from God.

She drew in her breath. Then she said aloud:

"That was what I felt...but for...him it was ...different."

With an effort she continued walking down the stairs.

As she reached the Hall her grandfather was being taken slowly with two servants to support him down the steps to the carriage that was waiting outside.

The coachman's whip had a bow of white satin ribbon on it, the horses' bridles were decorated with white flowers, and she could see as she came down the stairs a bouquet of white lilies lying on the small seat inside the carriage.

'Lilies for purity,' she thought, and remembered the crimson feathers in Evie's bonnet and the pink flowers she had seen being carried into the Supper Rooms to decorate the tables laid for two.

"Good luck, Miss!" the old Butler said as he helped her into the carriage.

"Thank you," Vanola replied surprised that her voice sounded so calm.

Then her crinoline had to be arranged before the servants could shut the door.

"Come on! Come on!" the Earl said impatiently. "We shall be late!"

"They cannot start the service without me, Grandpapa!"

"I dislike being late," her grandfather replied, "and your mother was always punctual. She soon learnt if she was not that I went without her!"

Vanola slipped her hand into his.

"Thank you, Grandpapa, for being so kind to me since I came to you."

"Kind? Of course I am kind!" the Earl said. "You are my daughter, are you not? I thought you would have made a better marriage—but Brook is a good man. He will take care of you."

Vanola knew once again he was thinking she was her mother and there was no point in contradicting him.

"Yes, Grandpapa," she said, "I am sure he will be very kind."

They went on down the drive which was long and winding. Then just before they reached the lodges at the end of it the horses came suddenly to a standstill.

"What is happening? Why are we stopping here?" the Earl asked sharply. "We are not yet at the Church."

Vanola wondered too.

Then as she bent forward to look out of the window the door was opened and a man wearing a mask looked in.

Vanola stared at him in disbelief and as she did so

he bent forward, picked her up from the seat on which she was sitting, and lifted her out of the carriage.

She gave a little cry of sheer astonishment as he carried her towards another closed carriage which blocked the drive in front of them.

On the box the coachman and the footman held their hands up in the old-fashioned gesture of surrender and she saw another man also wearing a mask and riding a horse was pointing a pistol at them.

The man who was carrying Vanola to the other carriage put her down on the back seat, and as he did so, she managed to ask in a frightened voice:

"What is . . . happening? What are you . . . doing?"

"Do not be frightened, everything is all right," he answered quietly.

Before she could reply, almost before she could realise that she had been taken from her grandfather's side, the carriage in which she was now sitting started off and was travelling at a tremendous pace out through the drive gates.

Then Vanola realised that it was not turning right towards the village Church where she was to be married, but left.

She leaned back against the soft seat of the carriage, feeling completely bewildered and unable to think what she could do about it.

She had been abducted, kidnapped, and yet why or for what reason she could not imagine.

All she knew was that the carriage was travelling so fast that it was difficult to think, and she was sure there must be at least four horses drawing it.

Then when she bent forward she could see that the two men in masks on horseback were riding ahead.

164

"Who are they, and what is happening?" she asked herself.

Then almost like a far-away note of music it seemed as if a tiny flicker of hope filled her heart like a light in the darkness of the night.

Vanola wondered what her grandfather was thinking and what was happening at the Church where Colonel Edward Brook would be waiting for her.

Then from the window she had a quick glimpse of a village green, a black-and-white Inn, and the horses were drawing to a standstill outside a small grey stone Norman Church.

As she waited, her heart thumping, the door of the carriage was opened and a man looked in. Now he was unmasked, and she saw he had fair hair and blue eyes.

She was certain at first glance that she had seen him somewhere before.

Then as he asked with a smile: "Will you please step out?" she remembered.

It was the handsome young man who was accompanying the Duke when he had come into Kate Hamilton's and having drunk with him at the Bar, they had both left the Saloon.

She felt her heart begin to beat with heavy, suffocating strokes. She stretched out her hand, and as she was helped from the carriage to the ground she heard faintly through the open Church door her father's music being played on an organ.

The young man offered her his arm and, as she held onto it like a lifeline in a heavy sea, he said again:

"Do not be frightened."

She wanted to tell him that she was not frightened,

165

only suddenly wildly excited, but her voice had died in her throat, and she could only look at him dumbly through her veil.

"You look very beautiful!" he said quietly as if to reassure her as he led her through the door and into the Church.

It was a small Church and the music from the organ seemed to fill it with the rhapsody of love that her father had played to her mother.

It filled her mind and her heart, and, as the man beside her drew her slowly up the aisle, she knew with a joy that seemed to make the whole Church glow with a light who would be waiting at the altar steps.

He was there and as she reached him the Duke put out his hands and touched hers. When he touched her she felt her vibrations join his, and they were one.

He did not speak, and there was no need for words.

Vanola only knew that her miracle had happened, her mother and her father had saved her at the last moment, and they were beside her telling her this was what they had always wanted for her.

Her fingers tightened on the Duke's, and as if he knew what she was feeling he looked at her for a long moment and she could see the love in his eyes.

Then they were both standing in front of the Priest and the Service began.

The Duke said his responses in a firm voice and with a sincerity that seemed to Vanola to vibrate within her heart.

As they knelt for the blessing she knew as she held tightly onto the Duke that God blessed them both because their marriage was sacred and Divine, and she need no longer be afraid of the evil to which she had so very nearly surrendered herself.

When they rose to their feet the Duke lifted her veil from her face to throw it back over the wreath of orange blossom. Then he looked down at her before he kissed her very gently on the lips, and she knew it was a kiss of dedication.

At the same time, her whole heart and soul leapt towards him, and she knew that she was his not only because of their love, but also because of the sacred vows they had made.

He did not offer his arm, but took her by the hand and led her back down the aisle, and she felt as if she walked on clouds, and the Church was filled not with empty pews but with angels who had watched their marriage.

The sunshine outside was caught in her eyes as she raised her face to the Duke, and as they walked down the short path towards the lych-gate he said:

"You are mine!"

She did not answer him because it was impossible, and only when they were in the carriage and driving off did she turn and say:

"Is it . . . true? Is it really . . . true that I am . . . married to you?"

"You are my wife!" the Duke said. "My darling, there is so much I have to say to you, so much explaining to do, but now I want only to kiss you, and make sure that you are real and I cannot lose you again."

Before she could answer, his lips were on hers, fierce, passionate, demanding, and she felt as if he carried her into the sky, and there was no need for explanations or for words.

She belonged to him, they were blessed by God, and they were one person.

*   *   *

Later, although time seemed to slip by in a flash, Vanola found they were staying at an exquisite house that was a little way off the Dover Road.

She was so bemused by the Duke's kisses and so utterly and completely content to be in his arms that there seemed no point in asking questions, or even enquiring where they were going.

Only when the sun had lost some of its heat did the Duke say:

"I do not want you to be tired, my precious one, and we are going to spend the night, or perhaps two nights, at a house I own in Kent."

"We shall be . . . alone?" Vanola asked quickly.

"Just you and me," the Duke replied.

"That is what I want . . . more than . . . anything in the world!"

As she went up the stairs and saw the two maids waiting for her at the top of them she wondered how she would manage without any clothes, except for her wedding-gown.

She was however still too bemused by her happiness to think of anything but the Duke, and only after she had bathed in scented water in a small Dressing-Room off her bedroom did she wonder if she wore her wedding-gown tonight what she would wear tomorrow.

When she entered her bedroom she saw lying on the bed a very lovely evening-gown of white and silver, and looked at it in surprise.

"To whom does that belong?" she asked.

"To you, Your Grace!" one of the maids replied.

168

"To . . . me?" Vanola asked.

"A large trunk arrived here from London earlier, Your Grace," the maid explained. "We unpacked what you needed and the rest is to go with Your Grace when you leave on your honeymoon."

Vanola drew in her breath, but she thought there was no point in asking questions.

Only as she went down the stairs to where she learned the Duke would be waiting for her in the Salon did she wonder why the silver and white gown fitted her so exactly, and where the clothes had come from.

Then she could think only of the Duke, and as she entered the room and the door closed behind her she saw him standing in front of the fireplace.

For a moment they just looked at each other, then he held out his arms and she ran to him as if she had wings on her feet.

He held her close against him, and she thought nothing could be more comforting or more wonderful than the feeling of security he gave her.

She lifted her face to his.

"I . . . love you!"

"And I love you!" he replied. "But for God's sake, my darling, never leave me again! If you did I could not suffer again as I have this last month thinking I had lost you."

"I . . . I did not want you to be . . . unhappy."

"Were you happy without me?"

She thought of the tears she had shed every night and hiding her face against him she said:

"I thought I had . . . died! Without you there was only . . . darkness and a world that was . . . not a world."

169

His arms tightened as he said:

"Now you are mine and nothing, my beloved, shall ever separate us again!"

Then he was kissing her and it was impossible to talk or think, but only to feel.

It was when dinner was finished—with wine that was like nectar and food which was ambrosia, Vanola thought that she had no idea what she ate—and they were alone once again in the Salon that the Duke said:

"My darling, I have to confess how ashamed I am that I should have insulted and hurt you as I did. It will be hard for you to understand, but if you love me, I want you to try."

"I do love you! I love you until nothing seems to matter now that I am your . . . wife."

He lifted her hand to his lips before he said:

"I thought as I was changing for dinner tonight that only Fate, which brought us together in the first place, could have saved us at the eleventh hour from losing each other, when now at this minute you might have been married to another man."

"I do not want to . . . think about . . . it."

"We will forget it for all time," the Duke said, "but first I have to know that you forgive me."

"There is . . . nothing to forgive."

"Yes, there is," he insisted. "I knew after you had run away what I had done, that I had not only hurt you but despoiled the music that means so much to us both, and which stands for the ideals that are often forgotten and defamed and the purity which, my darling, is you!"

There was a little pause. Then Vanola said in a hesitating voice:

"I . . . I . . . thought . . . perhaps because I had been

170

...associated with women like those at...Kate Hamilton's...you could never ...respect me as you might...otherwise have done."

There was silence and because she expected the Duke to speak she raised her eyes to his and saw the pain so poignant, so deeply etched in his face, that she cried out because she could not bear him to suffer any more.

"I should...not have...said that!"

The Duke's fingers tightened on hers, until they were bloodless.

"That is what I knew you were thinking," he said, "that is what has haunted me and taunted me until I thought I should lose my mind."

He kissed her forehead before he went on:

"How can I explain to you that because I have always been afraid of my marriage being utterly boring, I never associated you with the image I had of a conventional wife chosen for her suitability!"

He paused before he continued:

"To me you were something so apart that I could not connect the two, or think of anything except you held my heart, my body, and my soul and they were yours."

Vanola knew he was speaking as if every word was drawn from him, and from the pain he had suffered fearing she would never understand.

"I...understand what you felt," she said quickly, "because now I have seen the house in which my mother was brought up, I know how courageous it was of her to leave it to marry the man of whom my grandfather disapproved and thought...unworthy to be his son-in-law."

"Will you believe me," the Duke asked, "when I

tell you that never, for one moment, did I think you unworthy to be my wife? It was just that marriage seemed something banal and conventional, which had nothing to do with the ecstasy and rapture which you have given me ever since we met."

"But it is . . . true that you have . . . married me," Vanola said in a whisper.

"I have married you without asking you if you would do so," the Duke said. "I have married you in a manner which will shock your grandfather and perhaps cause a scandal amongst the Brook family. However, my friend Brooky will make things as easy as he can by explaining that we have loved each other for a long time, but through unforseen circumstances were parted."

"But he must not . . . tell Grandpapa that I . . . played at Kate Hamilton's," Vanola said quickly. "It would . . . upset him."

"That is something that neither of us will remember or talk about ever again," the Duke said firmly. "It would never have happened if I had not been so pigheaded that I did not understand that I first met you that you were what I had been looking for all my life, and thought I would never find."

He smiled and it seemed to illuminate his face as he said:

"I think when we listened to your father's lovesong we knew it was written for us, and we would never be able to feel what it expressed except together."

"Then you do . . . understand, and only you could have had it . . . played at our . . . wedding."

"I thought it would please you," the Duke said quietly, "and my darling, I have played it and played it to myself so often that I now know every note until

172

it is engraved on my mind and also on my soul."

Because the way he spoke was so moving Vanola moved a little nearer to him.

"I love you!" she said. "I love you so much that just as I felt at the Church that Papa was...beside us...so I feel now that his music is...vibrating on the air."

The Duke drew her closer, his lips found hers and she felt as if in his kisses there was not only the music and his love, but also everything which was beautiful.

They seemed to hold the sunshine, the moonlight, and the stars that were just coming out.

The Duke drew her to her feet and they went through the open window onto the terrace to look out onto the garden.

The last crimson and gold of the sun was sinking behind the trees. The first evening star was twinkling overhead.

It was so beautiful that Vanola gave a little cry, then she was holding onto the Duke to say:

"It is true! Tell me it is...true that we are...here together...that you love me...and I am your wife...and I need never be...afraid or alone again."

"You are mine!" the Duke replied, "and, my darling, this is real, this is what we both knew we have been seeking alone, and now there is so much for us to find together."

Then he was kissing her until she quivered in his arms, and she could feel his heart beating frantically against hers.

While what they had felt in Church was sacred and what they found beneath the stars was the ideal that was linked with her father's music, there was another side of love, and that too was part of the Divine.

* * *

A long time later Vanola could see the stars shining through the open windows from which the Duke had pulled back the curtains.

Now they seemed to glow like diamonds in the sable of the sky and there was a mystery about them which seemed to be echoed in her heart.

When the Duke made love to her there was music in the air, and the rapture and ecstasy they felt carried them up to the stars.

At the same time they were enveloped with the blinding light of the sun which swept through their bodies, burning away the fear and unhappiness they had both suffered.

She rested her head against the Duke's shoulder and felt his lips on her hair.

"I . . . I love you," she whispered.

"My precious, my perfect little wife!" he said. "I have not hurt you or made you afraid?"

"How could I be afraid of . . . anything while I am . . . with you?"

"That is what I want you always to feel."

"I am so happy, that I want to sing and dance on top of the mountains, to ride beside you over the grass of the steppes towards a horizon beyond which there will always be another horizon and you will never . . . never be . . . bored."

"That is exactly what we are going to do."

She looked up at him not understanding, and he asked:

"Where would you like to spend your honeymoon more than anywhere else in the world?"

She gave a little gasp. Then she said:

"Do you mean . . . ?"

"I mean my precious love," he answered, "that I

174

am taking you to Hungary. I want to hear your father's music in its rightful setting, and understand love as he did, and learn how to make you happy, as he made your mother."

"I am happy," Vanola said. "So wildly, unbelievably happy, but to be in Hungary with you would be the most wonderful, marvellous thing that could ever happen."

"That is what I feel too."

"How can ... you think of ... everything?"

"I think of you," the Duke said, "and I have had a lot of time to do so."

Because she wanted to comfort him she moved a little closer to him and said:

"I have not yet asked you how you managed to find those lovely clothes for me and have them waiting when we arrived."

"They are all things I arranged when I was desperate at losing you," he said, "and yet at the same time, some spark of faith that could not be quenched told me that by the mercy of God I would find you again."

"So you bought clothes for me."

"A *trousseau!*" he corrected, "and what is here is only a tenth part of it, my precious."

He knew she was still puzzled and he explained with a smile:

"When I went to see Mrs. Bates to find out for myself if you had really left your lodgings and did not intend to come back, she showed me your bedroom, and I saw hanging up the gown which you had worn when I first saw you, pointing a pistol at me, and ordering me to obey you."

Because she felt shy at the memory of it Vanola

hid her face against his neck and the Duke went on:

"I took it away with me, and, as I knew it fitted you, I ordered dozens of gowns in which I thought you would look more beautiful than I have ever seen you. Many of them are waiting for you in London when you go back, and we will also buy some more in Paris on our way home."

Vanola gave a little laugh of sheer happiness. Then she said:

"How could you be so . . . sure you would find me when I had given up . . . hope of . . . ever being with . . . you?"

"Completely and absolutely?" the Duke asked.

"I . . . I still prayed," Vanola answered in a hesitating voice, "that perhaps . . . by some miracle God would . . . bring us together."

"He has! He has given us our miracle, Vanola, and I intend that we shall show our gratitude, my dearest heart, by making sure than a genius like your father's is never again forgotten or ignored."

He paused, before he said:

"When I was alone and so desperately unhappy I thought the only reparation I could make for my stupidity was to help musicians to fame, and to revolutionise the Music World so that music does not only mean entertainment, but also inspiration to all those who listen to it."

"You understand!" Vanola said. "Oh, my darling . . . wonderful . . . husband, you . . . understand!"

"Only because you have taught me to do so," the Duke said. "We both of us have a great deal more to learn, and as you have already said, when we reach the first horizon, there will be another beyond it."

"You are so wonderful!" Vanola breathed. "How

176

could I have been so incredibly...lucky as to have...found you?"

Because there was a depth and a touch of passion in her voice which had not been there before, the Duke's lips found hers.

He kissed her until she felt the sun burning in her again, only more insistently, and she knew it complemented the fire she could feel on his lips which she knew consumed his whole body.

It was so exciting, so thrilling that it was a rapture that could only be expressed in music.

And as she felt as if the melody which had been playing softly while the Duke kissed her now became a crescendo of golden liquid notes rising in their hearts and bodies towards the stars.

This was love, this was the whole complexity, ecstasy and beauty of it.

"I adore and worship you!" the Duke exclaimed. "But my darling, I want to be sure you are mine. Give me yourself."

"I am...yours!" Vanola whispered. "Take me... oh...take me!"

Then as they were lifted on the swelling wonder of a love-song, up into the sky, the beauty and wonder of the night carried them on notes of celestial glory into the Kingdom of Love.

ABOUT THE AUTHOR

Barbara Cartland, the world's most famous romantic novelist, who is also an historian, playwright, lecturer, political speaker and television personality, has now written over 300 books and sold 300 million books over the world.

She has also had many historical works published and has written four autobiographies as well as the biographies of her mother and that of her brother, Ronald Cartland, who was the first Member of Parliament to be killed in the last war. This book has a preface by Sir Winston Churchill and has just been republished with an introduction by Sir Arthur Bryant.

Love at the Helm, a novel written with the help and inspiration of the late Admiral of the Fleet, the Earl Mountbatten of Burma, is being sold for the Mountbatten Memorial Trust.

Miss Cartland in 1978 sang an Album of Love Songs with the Royal Philharmonic Orchestra.

In 1976 by writing twenty-one books, she broke the world record and has continued for the following five years with twenty-four, twenty, twenty-three, twenty-four, and twenty-four. She is in the *Guinness Book of Records* as the best selling author in the world.

She is unique in that she was one and two in the Dalton List of Best Sellers, and one week had four books in the top twenty.

In private life Barbara Cartland, who is a Dame of the Order of St. John of Jerusalem, Chairman of the St. John Council in Hertfordshire and Deputy President of the St. John Ambulance Brigade, has also fought for better conditions and salaries for Midwives and Nurses.

Barbara Cartland is deeply interested in Vitamin Therapy and is President of the British National Association for Health. Her book *The Magic of Honey* has sold throughout the world and is translated into many languages. Her designs "Decorating with Love" are being sold all over the USA and the National Home Fashions League named her in 1981, "Woman of Achievement."

Barbara Cartland Romances is a book of cartoons. Seventy-five newspapers in the USA and in many other countries in Europe are also carrying her strip cartoons.